Dreaming in Quantum
(and Other Stories)

LYNDA CLARK

FAIRLIGHT BOOKS

First published by Fairlight Books 2021

Fairlight Books
Summertown Pavilion, 18–24 Middle Way, Oxford, OX2 7LG

A CIP catalogue record for this book is available from the British
Library

1 2 3 4 5 6 7 8 9 10

ISBN 978-1-912054-65-7

www.fairlightbooks.com

Printed and bound in Great Britain by Clays Ltd.

Designed by kid-ethic

For April and all those who love her

CONTENTS

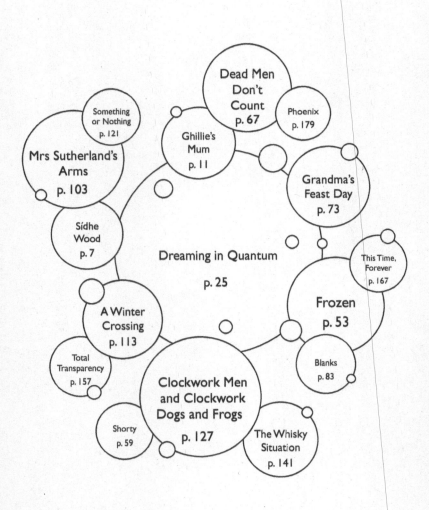

SÍDHE WOOD

When Saoirse Murphy's baby was found, it was the talk of the town. Everyone went on about it for weeks – how the poor mite was so lucky to turn up unharmed, pram and all, in the Sídhe Wood. Once the relief was done with, which took less time than you might think, Saoirse herself became the object of their gossip. Had someone *really* taken the pram while she sat on the bench by the wood's entrance? Or had she just left the baby there and wandered off, hoping a passing crow would take pity on her and whisk it away? She was only eating dry-roasted peanuts and reading a celebrity autobiography, couldn't have been that deeply absorbed, surely?

Connor Kelly was nowhere to be seen these days, that much was certain, the two-timing, baby-ditching bollocks. Maybe Saoirse just forgot she had a baby now, and went home to bake that batch of fairy cakes for her ma's church like she'd promised, mistakenly leaving little Sean there on his own, gurgling up at the ash trees, just like Jack was doing now.

(Only Jack was holding his feet and going red in the face, no doubt filling his nappy again, the little shite factory.)

Saoirse wasn't the brightest. Maybe she forgot and then felt embarrassed and didn't want everyone to know and so she made up the thing about looking away for a second and looking back to find Sean and the pram gone, taken by some unknown woodland kidnapper. Ciara peeked over the edge of her magazine at Jack again. He seemed happier out here. Cried all the time at home. Screamed his little lungs out. Ciara could sympathise on both counts: Jack's screaming, and Saoirse's shame. Ciara had once punched a nun in the tit at school, and she was still 'that wicked girl who hit Sister Claire' seven years later. And maybe Saoirse would rather be 'the girl whose baby was kidnapped' than 'the girl who forgot she had a baby and left him in the woods'. Although that was what they were saying about her in the village pub now anyway, of course. How else would you explain finding him only a few hours later, a few hundred metres from where she said she'd left him?

Ciara wadded a tissue and wiped the drool from Jack's chin. Ma reckoned he dribbled all the time because he was teething, but Ciara couldn't remember a time he hadn't done it and the little fecker still didn't have any teeth to show for it.

Anyway, these last couple of weeks, Saoirse had started saying wild things about little Sean. No doubt to distract attention from having forgotten him in the woods – why come out with such mad nonsense otherwise? First it was that Sean didn't laugh the same. Before he went missing, he'd had a throaty chuckle and now he had a light, reedy giggle. Or so she said. Ciara would be happy if Jack did anything other than grunt and fill his pants; Saoirse should count herself lucky.

Next it was that his eyes were the wrong colour, although noticing a laugh before noticing eyes just added fuel to the fire of Saoirse being unobservant enough to leave a pram in a wood. To be fair, Ciara could barely remember what colour Jack's eyes were – they were usually scrunched up with screeching or the effort of squeezing out a turd.

'It was a gradual change!' Saoirse had insisted when Ciara saw her at the post office yesterday. 'They started out brown like before and now they're all blue, look!' She'd pinched Sean's cheek so his eyes shot open and they did look blue, you had to give her that. Not that Ciara could remember what colour they were before. 'He sleeps for *hours* now!' Saoirse said, looking like she could do with some shut-eye herself. 'And he never cries, not even when his nappy's wet, it's… it's creepy!' And Saoirse had burst into tears, meaning Ciara had to take her to the coffee shop and get her a hot chocolate to calm her nerves, even though what Ciara really needed to do was go to the chemist and get some cream for Jack's cradle cap because he had a head like a baboon's ballbag.

At the coffee shop, Saoirse had broken down and said she thought it wasn't Sean at all. Ciara wondered if she'd be able to tell the difference if someone swapped Jack. It depended what they switched him out *with*, she supposed. A bag of flour might draw her attention, what with being significantly quieter. But one of those howler monkeys? She doubted she could pick Jack out in a line-up of those.

'What do you mean, not Sean?' Ciara had asked, trying to block out that awful gummy noise Jack made while he sucked on the rubber teat of his bottle.

'I don't know, he's just not my baby!' Saoirse wailed. 'Look at him – can you really tell me that's my Sean?'

Ciara looked him up and down, and she had to admit he looked different. The Sean Murphy Kelly she knew was a red, angry little thing with cradle cap almost as bad as Jack's – a flaky head and thin, patchy hair. He screamed for sixteen hours out of twenty-four, and during the few where he was awake and not screaming, he stuffed his pudgy fist in his mouth and chomped it like a cream bun. This little charmer had a full head of downy brown fluff, wide, unblinking eyes that appraised her just as calmly as she studied him, and a complexion usually only found on little girls on tins of old-timey sweets.

'Course it's him!' she'd protested, but she wasn't so sure, not really. Just because he showed up in the pram and the clothes didn't necessarily mean it was Sean, did it? It just meant this baby – whoever it was – was wearing Sean's clothes and sitting in his pram.

*

A breeze stirred the trees by the entrance to the woods. Ciara shivered.

Daylight was fading. Ciara pulled Jack's blanket a little closer under his chin and zipped up her own jacket. She wondered how much longer she should give it. A twig snapped behind her and she turned, although Jesus knows what she expected to see. A sídhe sneaking among the blackthorns, all long thin fingers and gossamer hair? There was just a fat brown bird hopping through the undergrowth with a blackberry in its beak. She turned back, half hopeful, half expectant.

The pram was still there, and so was Jack.

She settled back down to her magazine. Maybe give it another half hour.

GHILLIE'S MUM

When he was a baby, Ghillie's mother was mostly an orangutan. Like most mothers, she'd cradle him in her arms and blow raspberries on his belly, but unlike most mothers, she'd also change his nappy with her feet. In those early days, as far as he could recall, it was only at bath time she was other animals. A baby elephant to squirt him with water from her trunk, a porpoise to bat his rubber duck round the bath with her domed head, a dumbo octopus making him laugh with her big, flapping ear-like fins, and grasping his bath toys with her many arms.

Ghillie assumed everyone's mother was many things and so didn't worry about it at all for the first few years of his life, but when he started school, he realised his mum wasn't like other mums. And that meant he wasn't like other kids.

'Your mum had sex with a pig!' said Caspar, a boy in Ghillie's year, but far larger and with much harder fists. 'That's why she's all animals.'

Ghillie asked his mum about it when he got home. He didn't really know what sex was and he was worried it might make her cross if he asked, so he just parroted Caspar's statement to her and asked if it was true.

'Isn't it nice that he thinks I'm *all* animals?' she said. 'I'm not even sure I can do them all myself.' And she became a fat little Shetland pony and gave Ghillie rides round their living room, making the worn carpet worse than ever with her hooves. Ghillie kept the taunts to himself after that, because she didn't seem to understand anyway.

*

Parents' evening made the situation difficult to ignore. It was autumn and dark early, so Ghillie's mother was a panther, prowling alongside him, amber eyes mindful of danger. She led him over the crossing and up to the school gate, weaving through the assembled parents and children who'd stopped to chat on the playground before going in. Ginny McClaren's mum screamed and Ghillie's mum bared her teeth in response. Caspar elbowed his dad and they both stared, lips curled.

'Please, Mum,' said Ghillie and she became a racoon by way of apology as they went inside.

*

'I've had some concerns about Ghillie's language development,' said Mrs Rodney, Ghillie's English teacher. 'Although I think now I see the root of the problem.'

Mum was sitting on her tail on the little plastic chair, scratching her furry belly with her small black handpaws.

'Mrs Campbell! Would you at least do me the courtesy of being human while we speak?'

Mum became a naked, sad-faced woman, with dark rings round her eyes. 'It's Ms,' she said. Her hair was long and covered her breasts, and she drew one leg up against her chest to hide herself further, but several parents had noticed and were covering their children's eyes. Mrs Rodney was scandalised. She took off her cardigan and made Ghillie's mum put it on.

'I think it's time social services were involved,' Mrs Rodney said firmly.

*

Social services gave Mum a whole list of conditions she had to adhere to. She wasn't allowed to be animals anymore, under any circumstances, or they would take Ghillie away from her. She could no longer work as what she called an 'occupational therianthropist' (Ghillie didn't know what that part meant) and instead had to get a real job where she contributed to society. If she didn't, they would take Ghillie away from her. She nodded, her mouth a thin line, unlike any animal Ghillie had seen.

*

Ghillie's speech didn't get any better. If anything, it grew worse. He didn't have much to say to the tall, wan woman who made him porridge in the mornings, and returned from work each day greyer and greasier, smelling of chips.

'Can you not bring chips home sometimes?' asked Ghillie one day.

Mum shook her head. 'We have to throw them away at the end of the shift,' she said. 'You wouldn't want them anyway.'

'Why not?'

'The potatoes are old, diseased things, coated in grease to make them seem better.'

*

The next parents' evening was different and the same. Mum washed her hair, but it was still greasy and lank. It was like that all the time now. She wasn't animals anymore, not even when she was getting ready. Ghillie used to love that, when she crawled into her nightshirt as an otter and then transformed, arms sliding out of the sleeves like buds growing. But today she just buttoned her shirt with her boring human fingers and told him she hoped he'd been behaving. She put on flared jeans and a sheepskin waistcoat, and licked her hands to slick down Ghillie's hair.

When they made their way through the school gate, Caspar elbowed his dad, who snorted, saying: 'What is this, the seventies?' and several of the other parents laughed.

Mrs Rodney was different, though. Solemn, polite, concerned.

'Ghillie barely speaks at all now,' she confided, as if Ghillie wasn't there and didn't know. 'Does he speak at home?'

Mum was perched on the tiny plastic chair, knees almost to her shoulders, all awkward human angles. She shrugged.

'When he has something to say.'

'And you don't have anything to say at school, Ghillie?'

Ghillie's eyes felt too big for his head. He worried for a moment that he was becoming an owl, but Mrs Rodney just continued to stare at him patiently. Mum reached over and squeezed his hand, and he shook his head.

'Very well,' said Mrs Rodney, but she didn't look like anything was very well at all.

*

That summer, Mum ended up in hospital. She slipped and poured hot fat all over herself at the chip shop. As she hit the ground, she became a pangolin and rolled up tight to avoid the worst of the searing liquid. Her boss said it was unhygienic to be an animal in a food place, no matter what the reason, and he couldn't let her work there anymore.

'Will they take me away?' Ghillie asked, sitting on a big plastic chair by her hospital bed, legs dangling, not reaching the floor.

'No, no,' said Mum, reaching for him with her big band-aged mitt.

And she was right.

They took her away.

*

People assume all kinds of things about you when you're silent. That you're stupid. That you're smart. That you can't hear. That you can't communicate. That it's a religious thing. That it's an attention-seeking thing. Over the years, Ghillie heard them all. The religious thing was closest to the mark, although truth be told, his motives were far from holy. He'd made a vow to speak only when he had something worth saying, but he persisted with it because of how it infuriated people. Social workers, teachers, policemen, doorsteppers – they couldn't bear his silence. Sympathy turned to rage in a surprisingly short space of time, particularly if he didn't meet their eyes. It gave him a perverse sense of pleasure, saying nothing as they wheedled and cajoled, pleaded and threatened.

The Registry wasn't so bad once he got used to it. The dorms were noisy at night and some of the boys tried to taunt him into saying something, but he didn't have to put up with Mum's cat hairs on the pillow and there were never stray feathers floating in his soup. The dorm warden was a kind man with large strong hands and deep pockets that bulged with bags of peppermints and chocolate-covered fudge and jelly snakes. The peppermint taste got into all the other sweets, but it was preferable to fur and feathers.

The warden never asked Ghillie to speak, either, just ruffled his hair and gave him a sweet. He had an old black Labrador. The first time Ghillie saw it he half hoped it was his mother being sneaked in to visit, but of course it wasn't – she was in the Facility, probably for good. Unless she could stop being animals, which of course she couldn't.

*

Ghillie only visited her once during those years at the Registry. The warden took him. The Facility wasn't as nice as the Registry. Everything was painted pale lemon, intended to be clean and bright, but looking anaemic and sick. The foyer was nice, with red leather armchairs and a spiky green plant and a coffee table heavy with glossy hardcover picture books. But the foyer was separated from the rest of the Facility by a heavy door, a door that required the nurse to punch in a code on a keypad, before heavy bolts hissed back and it slid open. More of these doors separated the rest of the Facility's inmates from one another and from the world.

Mum was on a chair in the middle of a room with no other furniture except an identical empty chair opposite. The floor was tiled, white with non-slip ridges. The warden indicated the chair for Ghillie and then retreated to the corner with the nurse and a cardboard cup filled with coffee. As Ghillie approached the empty chair, he saw there was a circular drain right in the centre of the room. Very strange.

Mum's hair had gone from lank to dry, the ends split, wiry greying tangles tumbling to her shoulders over thin grey scrubs. She looked like an origami woman trying hard to stay folded.

As Ghillie sat down she glanced up briefly, gave him a twisted half-smile and then became, very suddenly, a full-sized adult rhinoceros. The speed and force of the transformation knocked Ghillie, chair and all, over onto his back. As he struggled to sit up, she was quickly a woman again, her papery clothes shredded, but the nurse was already rushing towards her.

'I'm sorry!' Mum shouted. 'Ghillie, I didn't mean—' and then she became a bird of paradise and swooped towards the ceiling, the plumes of her tail unfurling.

Ghillie couldn't respond, could only lie on the floor, rubbing the deep ache in the small of his back where the chair had butted into him and staring at the odd guttering that skirted the room, scooped-out hollows to guide non-existent liquids towards the central drain. The nurse tried to grab Mum, but she flew high, then swooped at the viewing window, smacking against the mirrored glass. She dropped to the floor, human and sobbing.

'It's these meds, it's these damn—' and she was a tiger, reddish orange and raging, but the nurse seemed unfazed and plunged a huge needle into the striped neck, pressing down on the syringe until it was empty. Even as she lapsed into unconsciousness, Mum continued to change, a mouse, a dog, a rat, a pigeon, a rooster, a chimpanzee, a trout, on and on, faster and faster, until they blurred together, a grotesque quivering mass of fins and fur and beak. As the orderlies wheeled her away and she continued to change weight and mass, Ghillie heard the gurney groan and squeak until they had disappeared through enough heavily locking doors. He was shocked and horrified. He'd never seen her like that before.

Maybe she could do all the animals.

'You see why we can't really have them in the community?' the nurse told the warden over Ghillie's head.

'What did she mean?' Ghillie asked, and heard the warden's sharp intake of breath. That was one of the gifts of silence. When you spoke, it was a moment. 'About her meds?'

The nurse looked uncomfortable for a second, then placatory.

'If she takes her inhibitors consistently, then everything's fine. If she forgets, or refuses... there are side effects.'

Why couldn't she just take her inhibitors? Ghillie thought, even though he didn't know what inhibitors were.

*

When Ghillie turned eighteen, the warden bought him a cake and decked the top with candles in little plastic holders. It was a celebration of his birthday, but also a goodbye party, marking the end of his time at the Registry. He didn't know where he would go when he left at the end of the day, but they'd given him a rucksack and a change of clothes and some money, so he supposed it would be all right.

All the Registry's current charges came to see him blow out his candles, the youngest around seven, the oldest due to leave herself in a month's time. Ghillie stared at the candles, watching the wax dribbling down towards the cake's iced surface, wondering if it was still good to eat if the wax got on there. The other charges sang the leaving song, but the warden didn't join in. His arms were folded, gaze fixed on the cake.

Ghillie drew in a deep breath, planning his exhale carefully so it would be powerful enough to extinguish the candles but wouldn't expel any spit, because everyone should get a share of the cake and they wouldn't want it with his spit all over it. But then he was a wolf, and instead of exhaling over the cake, he howled at the ceiling, a long, mournful noise, louder than any he'd ever made as a human.

The seven-year-old screamed, but the warden told him to shut up, SHUT UP, and that it was time for Ghillie to go now, and he helped Ghillie get his front legs through the straps of the rucksack as if Ghillie were still a person and ushered him outside, closing the door behind them on the hubbub of shocked children. He put his arms round Ghillie's neck like Ghillie had seen him do with the Labrador, and whispered in Ghillie's large ear:

'Don't let them put you in the Facility. You don't need to be in there.'

And Ghillie wished he had his human voice so he could thank the warden for everything, but he didn't, so instead he licked the salt tears from the warden's cheeks and ran off into the winter dark.

*

'Daddy, can't we come and see Nanny too?' Rocha was a marmoset, and her sister Bri, for reasons known only to herself, was a huge ox, licking cereal out of her bowl with a long mobile tongue, tail swishing like a metronome, large bovine eyes glued to the cartoon channel. Rocha dangled from Bri's horn, and once again Ghillie felt proud and jealous that they had mastered their gift so young. He could still only force out a few words while he was animal and his mum had never got the hang of it.

Ghillie buttoned his shirt.

'No, kiddos, Nanny doesn't need you two tromping around.'

Juhn was out front, mowing the lawn. It was early spring, and it didn't really need doing yet, but she got a little frustrated sometimes when the kids insisted on being animals all day. Firstly, breaking up a fight between a kangaroo and a Komodo dragon wasn't a fun way to spend a Saturday, and secondly, as she'd told Ghillie in the confessional space beneath their duvet one night, she often felt like the odd one out, the boring human.

'If you could have this, would you?' Ghillie had asked. 'Would you really?'

And she'd looked him in the eye and said, 'Yes,' with such conviction it reaffirmed for him that she was the right one, forever.

He pulled her away from the lawnmower and kissed her hair. 'If they get too much, just spray them with the hose.'

'Even in the house?'

'Even in the house,' he confirmed, turning back to her as he reached the gate. 'Kids are water-resistant!'

⁂

She was an elderly polecat, curled up in a wicker chair, brown mask flecked with grey. All her animals were old now. Ghillie picked up a photo from her dresser. It was the Home's last gala day. All the residents were in the swimming pool; in the centre Mum was a dolphin and everyone was smiling.

They had both been uncertain about the Home at first, fearing it was another version of the Facility, just with floral throw pillows and baskets of potpourri to veil the smell of formaldehyde. But there was no formaldehyde here and no locked doors, apart from at night and that was just because Mr Gibson was a nudist absconder.

As Ghillie put the photo back on top of the chest of drawers, she woke and became an aged python. She draped herself round his neck by way of greeting, then slid over to the bed and under the covers to become human, because even the most open-minded son would rather not see his seventy-five-year-old mother naked if it could be avoided.

'I've been practising something,' she told him. Her hair was snowy white now, though not as white as the owl Juhn had found snagged in a barbed-wire fence all those years ago, wing broken and bleeding.

'Have you?' Ghillie sat down in her armchair and leaned back. How shocked Juhn had been when the vet had told her: 'Actually, it's not an owl, it's one of them.' And then double shocked, when he had whispered in an aside: 'I could put it down for you if you like? Pretend we didn't realise?' And she'd rushed out of there with the half-conscious creature in a cardboard pet carrier and taken him home and waited for him to be a person again.

Ghillie's mum became a rabbit, nose twitching. Became human again. 'No, that's not right.' Ghillie waited as she became a miniature pig. He'd never understood how she could do such a range of animals. The kids could do it too, from vole to crocodile and back again with ease. He had to build up to something large, and even then, it was hard to hold. No shape was hard to hold for them, his daughters, his mother. Back as an old, old lady, she pulled the covers up to her chin and grimaced in frustration. 'That's not it either. I'm sorry, Ghillie, I'm becoming a useless old woman.'

'Becoming?' asked Ghillie with one eyebrow raised. She threw a pillow at him.

Juhn had told Ghillie off when he came out of his snow-owl delirium and described the transformation as 'becoming a person'. 'You're always a person,' she'd said. 'Whether you're a donkey, or a gibbon, or, I don't know, a naked mole rat, you're never not a person.' That conviction, even back then, before she knew him. And then the law was repealed, and so the state saw him that way too, a person. There were still plenty of people who didn't see him as a person, but their power was waning.

And just as he thought that, lying on the bed was a dragon – not a Komodo dragon, an actual dragon, with lustrous copper-coloured scales and golden eyes and horns and a frilled ruff of thorny scales round her throat. She opened her mouth and for a moment Ghillie thought she was going to burn him up, that she hadn't really forgiven him for abandoning her, that these last few wonderful years had just been her biding her time until she could get her revenge.

But instead she said: 'Pudding.' And collapsed back into a tired old woman.

'Pudding?' asked Ghillie.

'I said a word,' she said indignantly, pulling on her robe just so she could put her hands on her hips and glare at him. 'I said a word as an animal. You were so impressed when the girls did it, I thought I'd try it.'

'The dragon was impressive!' said Ghillie, and moved onto the edge of her bed and hugged her, laughing. 'You realise that when the girls hear about this they're not going to leave you alone until you do a unicorn?' He didn't think he'd ever hugged her with both of them human before. It was strange. She was soft, fragile, breakable, just like him.

And Juhn was right, in a way, but she had it backwards. They were never not animals, Ghillie and his mum, and that was the right way for them to be.

DREAMING IN QUANTUM

I try to keep the sound of my sobbing to a minimum, but I've woken Ida. She doesn't complain, just swings her legs over the side of our bed and pads across to turn the light on, then returns, laying long, thin fingers on my quivering shoulders.

'He was never going to just grow old, now, was he?' she says softly, intending to comfort me. I feel only fury.

Of course he was going to grow old. He was going to charm all the old ladies at the nursing home with that twinkle in his eye, and I was going to visit and read to him and sneak in tobacco for his pipe when the nurses weren't looking. When he was older still, I'd feed him soup, warm his cold, knotted knuckles with my small hot hands and remind him what a great man he had been. I close my eyes.

'This is the wrong dream,' I say aloud, eyelids flickering somewhere a million miles away.

'Frequency's right,' he says, and I realise I spoke just to hear him respond, to know that my reality is not this one.

'But it's too late. It's... after.'

I come round fully and start to sit up, but he waves me back down. The electrode pads on my temples chug out lines of data on the EMG, like a lie detector test. He notes a few peaks and troughs on his clipboard before removing the pads. I wriggle up the gurney a little, propping myself on my elbows.

'But you were in the right moment?' he asks. Initially I understood his fascination. First time you see yourself die, it's like being punched in the heart. Shortness of breath, dizziness. But you know what? When it happened to me, I got over it.

The crux of our study is that there are countless thousands of Mes out there, all going about their lives in their alternate worlds. When I see one die, it doesn't mean I've died. Just because I saw her die, just because I felt every bullet as it pounded into her body, doesn't mean anything. Nothing remotely like that will happen to me. She was a soldier. We obviously made very different choices.

*

Sounds strange, but I admire the fact that so many of Wheatley's alternates are quantum dream theorists. Like he's so singular of purpose that his desire for knowledge spans the worlds.

Truth is, I never really intended to join Wheatley's class all those years ago. I had no grand plan of becoming a theoretical physicist or working on quantum dream theory. It was barely a thing back then. Wheatley was the sole proponent; Hugh Denisoff had yet to make his genius known – and I'd never heard of either of them.

If it hadn't been for my ridiculous crush on Julian Bando, I'd probably be working in some research lab now, filling a thousand little test tubes a day with a tiny pipette. Or maybe I'd have been sent down the series of random pathways that led to me being alone on that battlefield, hiding behind an abandoned car, its rusted bodywork peppered with the bullets of enemy insurgents.

I only went on the trip to the open day at Imperial College because Julian was going. Most of my A-level physics class was there, but I just followed Julian from room to room, all moon-eyed, laughing hysterically at his pathetic jokes. I didn't care which lectures we attended. Back then I had no intention of taking physics any further, or studying in London, no plans beyond tricking Julian into touching my hand or drinking from my water bottle or leaning his leg against mine in the lecture theatre.

At the end of the day, I was tired, and Julian, initially flattered by my attentions, was tired of me. When he sloped into 'Quantum Dream Theory: An Introduction', I almost didn't follow, but I figured I could at least watch him from afar and maybe doodle some pictures of his aquiline profile to drool over later. What can I say? I was a boy-mad idiot back then. No wonder some of the other Mes branched off so dramatically.

So I sat well away from Julian, notebook and pen poised for a few hours' drawing, ready to let the dry words envelop me like a dust cloud. But then Wheatley took the rostrum. Old, but not ancient like many of the professors we'd seen that day, and despite his folder shedding notepaper onto the floor, he seemed relaxed and confident. He spent an age shuffling through that disorganised wedge of pages, unconcerned by the restless fidgeting spreading among the gathered students.

I glanced across to see Julian, a cruel smirk across his handsome features, moments away from heckling, and he wasn't alone. The room was turning. Yet Wheatley didn't panic or hurry. Eyes shining, his mouth quirked in an uneven grin as he struggled to find whatever starting point he was looking for. When he did, he brandished the sheet aloft triumphantly, clearly enjoying the amused relief this provoked in his audience.

My drawing never got beyond Julian's luxuriant hairline. My page instead became filled with notes I barely understood. I knew I wanted to know more, and became torn between never wanting the lecture to end and wanting it to finish immediately so I could race to the library and research all these new concepts.

Quantum dream theory isn't so radical and crazed as its detractors suggest. It just takes Everett's many-worlds interpretation and runs with it, posits that when we dream – particularly when we dream about ourselves and others we know – we're actually glimpsing some of those many worlds. Some seem strange to us because these worlds branched away from our own at some distant point, resulting in different technologies, flora and fauna. And of course, not all dreams are quantum. Some are just regular weird shit; our brains mixing together the events of the day and spewing them back out. Specialised techniques and technologies allow us to focus purely on the quantum dreamscapes and alternate selves.

As we dream of other Us, they dream of other Them. For quantum dream theorists, the terms 'I' and 'me' and 'them' and 'us' lose all meaning while simultaneously being imbued with an almost mystical significance. Them and Us and Me.

There were academic terms we could use, but try referring to the Quantum Dreamer and the Quantum Alternate Self and the Quantum Alternate Self from the Dreamer's Perspective and from the Self's Perspective with any kind of regularity and you're back to Them and Us before you know it.

*

I look at Wheatley over my ravioli, aware that I probably have tomato sauce round my mouth. The university canteen has no separate areas for staff and students, yet everyone self-segregates. Facing Wheatley across the table still feels weird, like I'm breaking some unspoken social rule. As the freshers nearby discuss their plans for the day, last night's alcohol coming off them in stale waves, I feel I should be sitting with them rather than Wheatley. Although we've been colleagues for several years now, part of me will always be his student. It's that part that asks:

'Can I be your plus one at the inaugural dinner?'

'You don't need me to take you, Jane,' he says, somehow eating a pizza, drinking a can of coke and reading a paper on shared dreamscapes among twins at the same time. No wonder I always feel like I'm riding his coat-tails. He even surpasses me at doing lunch.

'Aren't you going?' I ask, dabbing my mouth with a napkin. It comes away bright orange. I reach for the entire sheaf, cheeks burning.

'Free booze and a chance to tell everyone how great I am?' There's that twinkle the old ladies will love someday. 'Just try to keep me away.'

Tucking the paper under the edge of his plate, he stifles a satisfied belch, completely unselfconscious. Notices my frenzied scrubbing and smirks.

'You missed a bit.'

'Where?'

He leans forward to point and then, at the last second, indicates my entire face.

*

We've been using our state-of-the-art sleep lab for a few weeks now, even though it has yet to officially open. We're like naughty schoolchildren, Wheatley charming the receptionist into giving him the door code early, me bouncing on the adjustable gurney so its pristine white leather already has scuff marks from my trainers. Somehow it was important for us to get in there and play around before we got our interns and had to become Serious Authority Figures. Not that Wheatley was ever particularly good at that.

When I'd proposed my PhD thesis to him – 'Identifying Many-Worlds Branches in Quantum Dream Threads' – I was petrified. I knew I had stiff competition in the form of Hugh Denisoff, a brilliant young hobbyist who was being head-hunted by MIT but had his sights set on Wheatley. Denisoff, studying in his garage at home, had independently reached many of the same conclusions as Wheatley. I forget the precise details of Hugh's proposal, but it was far more complex than mine. He'd even suggested existing technologies to appropriate for QD experiments, some of which are now present in our lab. Seriously good, Nobel Prize-worthy stuff.

I'd expressed my concerns to Wheatley in his office. He was standing on a chair in order to blow clouds of stinking grey smoke out of the narrow opening of his single window. Once he'd finished his most recent exhale, he leaned back inside, still towering above me on the chair, and said:

'You realise I pick my PhD students?'

'Well, of course...' I stammered. Even after studying under him for four years, I was still slightly fearful. I had, at that point, yet to realise what an enormous softie he actually was. 'But Hugh Denisoff...'

'Fuck Hugh Denisoff. Don't give a shit about him.'

He closed the window with a slam to frighten away a fat pigeon that had perched on the sill, and got down from his chair. And that was that. Denisoff went with MIT, whereas I stayed with Wheatley and got down to business.

I had no idea what I was letting myself in for.

*

Ida. Her skin, her high cheekbones, her straight nose that could've been carved out of stone, the soft curves of her waist and hips. In this life, at least, I've only ever been attracted to men. Naturally I've seen dream dalliances with women, but Ida's different. Ida is the love of this other Me's life and I, the Me in this world, love her a little too, even though we've never actually met.

I thought Wheatley might be at least slightly interested in her, because her existence suggested further points of investigation regarding the development of sexual attraction. Did this Me meet Ida because she was already attracted to women, or was Ida the only woman she could ever be attracted to? If I met Ida's alternate in this world, would I be attracted to her?

When I tried to move down this mode of thinking, Wheatley was dismissive, almost annoyed.

'Different people stick different bits in different other people the worlds over. Absolutely nothing revelatory about that.' He detached the latest printout from the EMG and spread it on the desk.

'Forget her. This' – he pressed the sheet forcefully with his index finger – 'this is the event to focus on.'

The EMG's scribble showed closely packed, violently spiking lines. Intense brain activity for a surprisingly long duration, usually indicative of traumatic dreaming. That again.

Why did he care so much about that specific Him's death? By that point, soldier Me's demise was a distant memory. I could barely recall her expression as she sank to the ground one bright, sunny day, bullets zinging into the earth around her even as she lay there on the warm grass, cooling.

I didn't say anything, though. You don't question your heroes, do you?

*

'Blood everywhere. And footprints. They're...'

'Don't worry about those for now. Can you see the body?'

'Yes.'

I look around his home first, stalling. It's generally the same – white walls and wooden floors, Scandinavian mini-malist design ruined by his inability to keep anything tidy.

Books overflow the shelves, stacked on the floor, on the irregularly shaped artisan coffee table, on the breakfast bar. Other Him has more awards than he does. Some weird shapes, strange organisations and fields of study I'm not familiar with. Perhaps they don't exist here.

The man's face down, head propped against his outstretched arm. He's only just got home, because he's still wearing his lab coat. He's balding, the greyish-white hair round his temples flecked with blood. His stomach has been slashed with a serrated blade, leaving a jagged tear, guts spilling onto the blonde wood. Bile rises in my throat, in real life and in the dream.

'Jane?'

'Sorry. It's—'

'Jane. It's not me, remember?'

But it is. It's Professor Wheatley, stiff and glassy-eyed, still warm in his cool apartment.

'Have *you* dreamed this?' I say.

Then I wake, and there he is, standing at my shoulder with his notebook, pens tucked behind his ear. Dead and not dead, like Schrödinger's cat.

'Not exactly. Just seemed to be the way things were going.'

'Maybe we can put you under later?' I suggest, sitting up, swinging my legs over the side of the gurney. 'See if we can find out what led up to this?'

'Maybe,' he nods. 'Why don't you just go over my notes for now, see if you spot anything?' He smiles, and I take the notes from him, already reading, not even bothering to say goodbye.

*

I keep replaying that smile. There was sadness in it. I should have seen it.

*

I don't know what to wear for the inaugural dinner. Dressing to attend things with Wheatley is always difficult. If I'm too glamorous (which admittedly is unlikely, but it *could* happen) there'll always be simplistic minds dismissing me as arm candy. If I dress as myself, I look too much like I'm still his student.

I don't know how to dress in a way that properly represents our relationship. Defining it is difficult enough. Am I his protégée? I suppose, but to me that implies something grander and more formal than the reality. A protégée would mean him taking me to a mountaintop like I'm the lion cub and he's the wise old monkey, holding me aloft for all the other physics bods to see. Which would only actually happen if he planned to drop-kick me into their midst for a laugh.

I find a mauve hooded dress screwed up down the back of the radiator. Haven't worn it in years and it smells of mildew. I smooth it, because ironing is intolerable, and hunt for a suitable pair of trainers. Why fight that student/teacher vibe? It's always going to be there.

Afterwards, I run a bath. I don't know how I can be so tired when my job involves so much sleeping, but I'm exhausted. I use supermarket own-brand bubble bath, because I refuse to pay a small fortune for a bottle of scented froth. Wheatley likes that. Not my bubble bath specifically; he's never seen it. But the fact I buy own-brand stuff. Speaks to his socialist sensibilities while he puffs on his burley tobacco.

*

I'm sitting on the sofa of what I now know is our apartment. Ida has her arm round me. We're both wearing bathrobes. My eyes are red from crying, lips chapped, face puffy.

I flit between first and third perspective when I'm dreaming. Not everyone has that – not in quantum dreams, at least. It's strange to look down on another You like some disembodied god. This Me has longer, blonder hair. Looks like she knows her way around a pair of straightening irons too.

A man is opposite us. I realise with a start that it's Julian; older, stubblier and with shorter hair, but unmistakably him with those heavy-lidded eyes and that fierce eagle nose. I recognise him, but Other Me doesn't seem to. Nothing unusual in that. I've never met Ida. She could've died in infancy in this world, or moved abroad, or she could live just one street away and a thousand tiny obstacles have forever kept us apart.

Julian holds a notebook and paces. He's wearing a long, dark overcoat and sensible black boots. It seems he's here in some official capacity: police or a private detective. He looks far more serious than he ever did when I knew him. Not that I ever knew him.

'I don't see what else she can tell you,' Ida is saying, her mouth a grim line. Other Me remains silent, just sniffles and glances at the door like she's willing him to leave.

'To be honest,' Julian says, 'it's not *your* Ms Jones I have questions for.'

And he looks right at me.

*

I sit up, spluttering. I've dozed so long and drifted so deep my mouth is below the waterline. My bubbles have dissolved into a sickly-sweet floral scum. The pads of my fingers are wrinkled and wizened, like the future Wheatley I daydream about nursing. I leap out of the bath swearing and run, dripping, to my bedroom.

Hurriedly towelling dry, I snatch up my phone. Quarter past eight. The inaugural dinner has already started. I was meant to be at Wheatley's for seven. He won't have waited.

Piling my wet hair on top of my head, I stick it through with grips to create some semblance of style. As I wriggle into my dress, still damp and hot from the bath, the armpits immediately darken with sweat. I cram my moist bare feet, soles uncomfortably dusted with carpet fluff, into my trainers and run.

By the time I reach the university, they're starting the main course. I make my apologies, breathlessly squirming into my seat, expecting Wheatley to be holding court at the head of the table. He isn't. Assuming he's stepped out with his pipe, I attack my butterfly chicken as soon as it arrives, splashing myself with lemon sauce within seconds, naturally.

When the waiters and waitresses – mostly students trying to claw back some of their astronomical tuition fees – come to collect our plates, Wheatley's still nowhere to be seen. I lean across to my neighbour, a red-faced man with crinkly black hair who I think I recognise from the chemistry department.

'Has Professor Wheatley been here at all?'

He's focused on the arse of the waitress attempting to retrieve his dirty cutlery. The fork's just out of reach, maybe accidentally, maybe on purpose. He doesn't move it closer, preferring to watch her lean. I repeat myself, and he answers without looking away:

'No. Never showed.'

The dessert is warm chocolate brownie with clotted cream, but I don't wait.

*

The lights are on in Wheatley's apartment. That sends a shiver down my spine, even though it's stupid. It's probably just Doris, the semi-retired lady who comes round at intervals to dust his shelves, feed his fish and snoop through his books and magazines. Sometimes she opens his mail under the pretence of separating the junk from the important stuff. Bound to be Doris. Darkness is falling, and my shiver has more to do with the rapidly dropping temperature than any real sense of foreboding. I left my jacket at home.

I cross the street and ride up in the small, brightly lit lift. It's made by a company called Schindler and whenever I end up in the lift with someone else, they point this out, usually making some kind of weird *Schindler's List* pun in the process. I hate those 'jokes' and I hate being in that lift with people. Today there's no one in the lift. No one in the whole building, it seems. Every corridor silent. Quieter than silent. Sucking in noise like a greedy calf at its mother's udder.

The door to Wheatley's apartment is open. There are deep gouges in it like someone's slashed it with a serrated blade. The quiet is here too, unsettling, like it's masking something deadly. A silencer on an executioner's pistol. My spine does that thing again, like it's trying to shake off loose quills.

I should probably just stay where I am, call the police, report a break-in. No need to go inside; I can already see something's up.

But it's not enough. I have to know, to know for sure. I pause. You might think that, in my line of work, it's tough knowing whether you're in a dream or not. But for the most part it isn't. It's hard to describe, but in the vast majority of dreams, everything feels just slightly off. Even when the dream initially feels real, that feeling rarely lasts long, because you'll quickly notice your perspective is strange, or you've changed location four times in the last two minutes – small things which leap out at the astute dreamer. But right now, for the first time, I'm having real trouble.

I mean, it feels real, but the gouges? A serrated knife...?

Threads are how we know we're in a consistent alternate world. They can include large details, like Other Jane's ongoing relationship with Ida, or small things, like walking past the same postbox every time you take a certain route. The more you dream, the more you learn to look for these anchor points. The EMG can look for them too. I'm not a neurologist, but I can read the waves the EMG kicks out without really knowing what they mean, y'know? They can tell me whether the dreamer's genuinely in the right place, or just thinks they are.

My PhD study aimed (and ultimately failed because it was ludicrously ambitious) to determine whether you could compare our world to these alternates and figure out the exact branching moment. The thing that stopped Them being Us and made them Them. Fortunately, my thesis was lauded as a stepping stone to further study rather than condemned as a failure, and we're finally getting closer to answering its questions. We've been able to return to specific alternates repeatedly, plot their timelines, see how they differ from ours. But what we've never had, never even come close to, is crossover.

Alternates are just that. They are alternative possibilities that played out somewhere else. They can't predict our futures, or show us our pasts, because they aren't *our* futures or pasts.

Until this.

Whatever this is.

It isn't anything. Some kid with a knife, wanting to ruin something for someone else. The door, I mean. The way they carved the door. Wheatley will be fine.

I take a deep breath and push the door. It swings open slowly, but real-world slowly. In dreams things feel like they're moving at normal speed, when actually they're going slower. Something to do with the brain being unable to gauge time properly without physical cues. As I said, I'm a physicist, not a neurologist. I deal with the theoretical and the quantum, not the messy stuff.

Messy stuff.

Messy stuff is an understatement. It's much worse than in the dream, more like a tornado has blasted through the apartment. His books are scattered everywhere, cracked spines and ripped pages. The curtains are torn – don't look – the curtains on one side of the dual-aspect room are torn down. The others flutter in the breeze from the window that for some reason has been smashed out into the street.

He's lying differently to the other him. Don't look. Face up. Eyes staring at nothing. Injuries are the same though. Multiple slashes with a serrated blade. Clothes slick with blood. Floor slick with blood. Blood. Don't look. Lots of blood. Don't look.

I looked and now it's all I can see.

Blood.

Stop looking at the blood.

I take out my phone and call the police. I have a strange, disconnected feeling, not unlike seeing through the eyes of an alternate. I think about how we've been trying to push our alternates, trying to get them to do things, to see if we can make a difference to their lives, to their threads. When we started that, it seemed like a violation. Forcing my will on someone else. But now I realise it's more like a hive mind, all the other Yous across the many worlds giving this You a nudge in the right direction. I think it was other Janes telling me not to look – maybe Janes who had never met their Wheatley but knew my pain regardless; maybe Janes with their own Wheatleys, glad this dream wasn't their reality. I like to think all of us made that phone call together.

*

The police arrive. One is a tall, thickset man, not Julian. The other is a small, brunette woman, also not Julian. I don't really know why I expected Julian at all. This world's Julian isn't a detective. Last I heard, he was an investment banker.

I'm not crying, which is good because I don't have an Ida to comfort me. The thickset man disappears into Wheatley's apartment, notebook in hand. The woman stands with me in the hallway as I pretend there's no dead body through the wall behind us.

'How well did you know the deceased?'

I'm shocked by the impact of that word, the finality of it, doubly shocked by the sob that escapes my lips.

'I'm sorry,' the policewoman says immediately, patting my arm. 'I'm so sorry.'

'The window's broken outwards,' the policeman calls through to us. I'm too busy crying and the policewoman has nothing to add, so after a moment he returns to the corridor. 'The window's broken outwards,' he repeats, oblivious to my misery. 'Anything missing? Could be something significant was thrown out during the altercation.'

Altercation. An altercation is when someone queue-jumps and you give them a piece of your mind. Or when a kid's football keeps hitting your windows so you take it and then they egg your front door. Whatever happened to Wheatley was no mere altercation. Instead of saying that, I say something that sounds like: 'Mmmmmihdunno'. I sense some looks going on over my bowed head as the officer admonishes him with her eyes. He leaves us again, and I hear him using his radio, requesting that forensics search the street below as well as the apartment itself.

'Anyone you'd like to call?' the officer asks.

There is, but he's lying on the floor with a gash in his belly. I shake my head and press at my eyes, taking deep breaths until I have enough air to speak.

'Can I just go home? I really need to sleep.'

*

I want to sleep, but I can't. For days I just lie on my bed and cry and picture Wheatley, alive and dead, but not like Schrödinger's cat. I get up now and again to answer the phone, usually the police with no leads and no further questions, keeping me updated on the fact there are no updates. Sometimes while I'm up I water the plants, or make hot milky drinks in the hope of sleep that never comes.

When I do eventually sleep, it's dreamless, like all the worlds have ended.

What if he's gone from all the threads? What if I never see him again?

*

Julian Bando has me by the shoulders and he's shaking me. It's an alarming point to enter a dream, and for a moment I'm afraid, casting around desperately for Ida, for a potential weapon, for a way out.

'Jane!' he shouts into my/her face. 'Other Jane! Do you hear me? Do you see me?'

She shakes her head as I nod mine, but I just keep right on nodding and eventually she does too. My heart races. Or perhaps it's hers.

He stops shaking us and gets off the bed.

'I'm sorry,' he says, and I know he's speaking to Other Jane for the moment. 'I needed to make contact and that was the way Wheatley suggested.'

My ears prick up at that.

'Wheatley's dead,' one of us says. Maybe both.

'Here, yes,' he replies, sitting on the silk-covered stool by the make-up table. Must be Ida's choice. Unless Other Me has very different taste in decor. 'In my world, Wheatley's very much alive.'

'Your... your world?' she says.

'You're from another thread?' I tack on the end.

Julian grins wickedly and I'm temporarily reminded why I found him so irresistible in sixth form.

'Yes,' he says. 'My Wheatley developed a technique to transmit willing volunteers – in this case, me – into alternate worlds.'

'You've seen other worlds?' Other Jane and I are working in tandem now, pulling together towards the same goal.

'Only this one. Anyway,' he suddenly grows frantic, 'we're wasting time. I have to tell you something before—'

I wake, breathless and disoriented, like I just straddled three worlds in one brief dream.

*

The glass in the street, fragments from Wheatley's broken window, contained traces of Wheatley's blood, suggesting it was the murder weapon that was thrown from the window. It was never found, indicating that the murderer retrieved the knife shortly after the murder was committed. So why fling it out the window in the first place? The knife's jagged blade suggested a ceremonial weapon of some kind, possibly carved from bone or wood. The murderer had employed considerable force and ferocity, indicating they were large and male. At least six foot five and upwards of nineteen stone. TV wrestler territory. Yet no one had seen a large man enter or leave the apartment block and there was nothing on the building's CCTV.

I look up the case online and find something else. Chatter on unsolved murder forums about a strange hole in the wall of the level below, knife gouges in the staircase leading up to Wheatley's floor. Crazed conspiracies abound. If any of that's true, the police are sitting on it, preferring to keep asking me unanswerable questions. Do I know anyone fitting that description? Is there anyone who might have a grudge against Wheatley? I'd hoped a little research would help, that it'd jog something into place, but now I'm just left with the strange feeling that the answers aren't in our world. I close my laptop. Time for investigations of my own.

*

Wheatley's crabbed handwriting lines sheets and sheets of EMG printouts. Some are mine, some are volunteers', but most are his own. That throws me. He's been studying himself without me. How long was that going on? A good few weeks if these notes are anything to go by.

I flip back to where he first found the thread he was so fascinated by, the thread that ultimately foretold his death. But there's nothing unusual. No great revelation. His notes simply say: *New consistent thread. Follow at this frequency*, with the frequency circled and an arrow to the event start point.

There are general observations about the similarities and differences between himself and this alternate, matching up of acquaintances, deviations from significant life experiences, the usual. And then, after about two weeks of this, in a different pen and large blocky capitals rather than the usual scrunched scrawl:
FIRST CONTACT.

Had Julian Bando spoken to him directly too? Was that why he'd been so interested in my alternate's position in this thread? Julian had popped up in other threads, so although I'd never told Wheatley about my crush, he knew of Bando's existence, was aware he was an acquaintance in this world. I swig some apple juice from the carton and pull my knees up under my chin. If only Wheatley had told me what he'd found.

Maybe I should phone Denisoff and tell him a vacancy's opened up in the department. He'd want to be the leading expert in QDT, wouldn't he?

I don't.

*

I'd be lying if I said there wasn't a tiny glimmer of excitement attached to Wheatley's death. Thanks to Wheatley's secret-squirrel activities and our general studies, we had stacks of date-stamped recordings of our lucidity sessions. Indisputable records of us describing the circumstances of alternate Wheatley's murder and subsequent investigation. Actual evidence supporting quantum dream theory's descriptions of the links between the worlds. The makings of a career-changing study.

I hated myself for seeing it that way, for seeing Wheatley's murder as a stepping stone towards fame and glory. I'd give a thousand Nobel Prizes for one more lunchtime chat with Wheatley, but that didn't make me hate myself any less.

I suppose I should have been the one to make funeral arrangements, but I left it up to the department. His parents were dead; his sister, also a brilliant physicist, had killed herself some years earlier.

The plan was for me and the Dean to give the eulogy. I told him I was writing it, but really I was spending every moment at the lab, combing back through our research, putting myself under, trying to find that alternate Julian Bando who spoke to me. Every time I came out in the wrong place, the wrong time, the wrong thread. I glimpsed Ida and Other Jane making love, trying to find comfort in each other despite Jane's grief; an other-world Julian Bando preparing to travel between worlds, doing meditations and mental exercises I only half understood; Doris being the one to find the body, freaking out about the blood, taking the opportunity to stuff her pockets with valuables before the police arrived. No Wheatley, no revelations. Perhaps if there'd been someone I could ask to monitor me, to adjust the frequency manually and push me into the right thread, I would have found the truth sooner. But there was no one I trusted – not in this world, at least.

*

It's the worst possible moment to get the giggles. The faculty is out in force, sombrely dressed, faces arranged into masks of solemn respect. Many of them are probably irritated that a state-of-the-art lab is being frittered away on a recently qualified doctor of physics when neurology could take it over, but they're hiding it well. I'm wearing a calf-length black dress and even proper shoes – patent brogues with grey laces.

To my left, the cafeteria lady snuffles quietly into a wadded-up tissue. Wheatley used to flirt with her to get bigger helpings.

The wood of the pew, rubbed shiny from countless other hands gripping it like mine are now, grows warm beneath my clenched fists. But my tension isn't down to suppression of grief, it's due to restrained laughter. For some reason, when I saw Wheatley's coffin, the sweet-smelling white flowers lining the stage, the assembled mourners, the tragic drone of the organ, the photo of him in his favourite tweed jacket with the suede elbow patches (such a cliché), I kept expecting that horror movie moment.

I could picture it exactly. A clawed hand bursting through the organ and the organist, bringing the music to an abrupt end. He'd clamber through the mess of brass pipes and antique wood, Wheatley's killer, cackling that I was next while two little girls turned a skipping rope and sang a creepy refrain. He'd be wearing a striped jumper and a fedora and have a face like a melted candle and he'd have been travelling across the dreamscape long before any of us.

I desperately want to tell Wheatley because I know he'll find it funny, and then I remember he's lying stiff and disfigured in that cold casket and the hilarity melts away in an instant and I'm numb again. I'm reminded of the soldier's face as she fell. Blank. Like her death meant nothing, because whoever there was to miss her was gone already. If the killer slashed me with his claws right now I'd be the same. Cut to ribbons, feeling nothing.

The music ends, and I sink back into my seat as the Dean takes the stage and mumbles platitudes about a man he never appreciated nor understood.

*

'I don't know why it's latched onto him,' Julian Bando is saying over a glass of red wine. 'All I know is I arrived here too late. It'd already moved on.'

They're in the dining room, sitting round a circular table. Jane still looks shell-shocked, cheeks glowing with an unhealthy fire, possibly due to the wine.

'Why don't you just follow it?' Ida asks, topping up Jane's glass, then her own.

There are candles on the table, not the only light source, but the main one. Late evening.

'I can't recreate the shift' – he looks pained – 'and there's no Wheatley here to help me. I'm stuck here.'

'What about Hugh Denisoff?' I ask.

'Jane?' Julian stands up, bracing himself against the table, leaning into Other Jane's face. His sleeve is in the melted wax of the candle, dangerously close to the flame, but he doesn't notice.

*

'Jane?'

My head is lolling back over the pew, my mouth wide open. I might've drooled a little. This may be the worst thing I've ever done. Even the neurologists are giving me black looks of disgust and they're no fans of Wheatley. I wipe my mouth with the back of my hand, then dab at my dry eyes, trying to indicate that falling asleep at a funeral is just some bizarre part of my grieving process. Truthfully, missing someone *is* exhausting.

I manage to make my speech without yawning or sniggering over visions of B-movie monsters. People cry and laugh in the right places. Afterwards we decamp to the university dining hall for the wake. It's done out much the same as for the inaugural dinner, but with a buffet along the back wall and caterers and waiting staff from an external company, allowing the students to attend and pay their respects.

Or get smashed on free wine. Some people have no sense of decency. Wheatley liked those people best. I make small talk for as long as I can stand, then yoink a bottle of whisky from behind the bar while the barman's distracted making a complicated cocktail for that lecherous dickhole from chemistry. I walk quickly to the staff toilets with the bottle down at my side as if that somehow disguises it. In my locked cubicle I sink to the floor on the cold white tiles to drink and cry until I vomit.

*

The first blow to the toilet cubicle brings me round. The metal stall crumples and gives with a grating sound, the wall distorting like a frying pan taking on the outline of a cartoon character's face. If I'd been sitting upright rather than slouched over the porcelain bowl, I'd be out cold on the floor right now. Or worse.

I see its feet move beneath the stall, but can't take the sight in. It has four, and they are somewhere between reptile and feline. The claws are impossibly long, and as it braces itself for a second lunge, the rear ones leave deep gouges in the tiles. It seems inevitable that it's going to spring into action, smash through the cubicle and slash me to pieces like it did to Wheatley. I hug the base of the toilet and wait for death, feeling nothing.

But the creature stops. Sniffs towards the toilet door. I see its nose to the ground, broad and wolfish, but scaled, hairless. It presses itself against the gap under the door, a wide head on a longish neck, too vast to fit underneath. I can only be grateful for that, as slaver drips from its massive jaws. It manoeuvres, turning to fix me with an iridescent compound eye. I know now what Wheatley meant when he wrote FIRST CONTACT. My guts freeze. It's hard to breathe. I can't even find the strength to pull all my fragile, slashable limbs out of view.

I hear the outer door open, hear Julian Bando call: 'Jane?'

'Don't come in!' I shout, but it's too late; the creature's attention has shifted away from me and towards him. I shake off the nothingness, brace myself against the leaning walls and kick the toilet door open hard, into its side. It screams, so I kick it in the head with all my might. It blinks, and opens its jaws, drawing itself back and raising its claws to attack. I fall back against the stalls in my desperation to put distance between it and me. Julian yells to regain its attention. He's drawn some kind of weapon – a tranquiliser gun – and he fires it at the creature, but it's running, running straight for him and its claws scrape the tiles and it's jumping over and past him and he's firing and the creature grunts and then there's the strangest sound, like the sensation when your ears pop, but outside, in the world, and then there's only silence. And it's that weird silence like at Wheatley's apartment, that active, hungry silence, intent on drinking in any noise around it.

For a moment I can't move, can't take in the fact that this is actually happening, that this isn't a dream or a drunken hallucination. Eventually, I hear Julian cough, and with a great effort of will, heave myself to my feet. I jerk my fingers away from the bent metal of the stall, blowing on them. It's blistering hot.

Julian is in the open doorway, surprisingly intact. He's put the weapon back in its holster and is holding a handkerchief over his face. He's examining the wall – or the hole in it, straight through into the neighbouring corridor. I go to lean through, but he pulls me back.

'Heat'll melt your face,' he says, voice muffled by the handkerchief. I notice the edges of the hole then: the concrete of the wall, several inches thick, reduced to glass. Fragments of glass and concrete are in the corridor outside, but of the creature there's no sign.

'Where'd it go?'

'On to the next one.' Julian looks grim. He tucks his hand-kerchief away and starts walking briskly back out into the corridor. 'I need to get there.'

'Wait, what was that thing?'

He stops, turns on his heel and gives me a grin that would have melted my heart ten years ago. 'Damned if I know.'

*

'He wants us to meet him in Edinburgh.' Julian pockets his mobile and folds his arms.

'Edinburgh?!'

'It was the first destination he could fly into.'

'Whatever. He just wants to start as he means to go on – getting us running round after him.'

Julian's made himself at home pretty quickly. Every surface in my small flat now has a different blue overcoat on it. How many overcoats can one man own? Eighteen-year-old me would've danced for joy at the prospect of Julian Bando sleeping on the sofa, but I just want him out of my hair. I'm not looking forward to working with Hugh Denisoff, but if it gets rid of other-world Julian and his overcoat collection, it's worth it.

Julian's theory is that a Wheatley in one world did some-thing to seriously piss this monster off and now it has a vendetta. After a close call with the creature and his own Wheatley, Julian tracked down Hugh in Ida and Other Jane's world to ask for help crossing over to mine. He's eager to meet this world's

Denisoff too, as if he'll have some spectacular insights about the creature. I want to remind him that I fought the creature off with only a toilet door, but it seems egotistical to bring that up. At least the sleep lab has been renamed the William Wheatley Dream Research Laboratory, so Denisoff won't get any ideas about who rules the roost there, even after I'm gone.

Speaking of gone, the creature seems to have moved on from this world. I skim the local news for strange animal attacks, mysterious vandalism involving serrated knives, anything that seems off, but there's nothing. Julian says he needs to move quickly, needs to contain it before it kills more Wheatleys.

I tell him I agree, that I'm going with him next time he crosses over because I'm chasing the creature, but really I'm chasing Wheatley. If I can see him in another world, I know I can save him; I know I can slay the beast. I try to ignore the mocking inner voice pointing out that the Wheatley who survived had a Julian, not a Jane. The Jane in that world was the wrong Jane. Hugh Denisoff may have taught himself quantum dream theory, but I've taught myself survival. I've taught myself to use my alternates to help me and others, to communicate across worlds.

I close my suitcase as Julian stands in the doorway. He watches over me a lot. Says his Wheatley told him to. When he says that I have the strangest sensation. Sad and happy and terrified. Too many feelings for one body, like straddling three worlds, all of them jostling beneath my feet.

In all these possible worlds and possible lives and possible deaths, one thing is certain. I won't die empty like that soldier.

FROZEN

'If it's alive, how comes it never moved?'

The small mitten reaches out, hovers over the icy snout, then withdraws.

'It only moves when no one's looking, stupid!'

The mitten returns, trembling. A slightly larger gloved hand knocks the mitten aside and scuffs at the sheen of frost, thumb working in circular motions to uncover the muscled leg beneath. 'And if it i'n't alive, how comes it never melts, even in summer?' Big said.

This last is said triumphantly. The larger one is obviously an authority on this sort of thing. But the smaller one is not so easily cowed.

'It i'n't *ice*,' the small one says scornfully. 'It's marble or summink.' It's the small one's turn to look triumphant. The large one looks confused. The only marbles he knows are made of glass and click satisfyingly when you flick them together. He can't let the little one realise that, though. Smirking, he lands on a solution.

'If you're so sure it's just marbles, turn your back on it, 'n' close your eyes.'

'I will.'

'Go on then.'

'You gotta do it too.'

'All right.'

'Come 'n' stand with me, then.'

'I'm not going all the way over there like a *baby*. I'm gonna stand right near it and do it.'

The small one's mouth drops open. It's just a statue, of course, but still. There's always a risk. Obediently, she turns her back and closes her eyes.

The large one waits until he's certain the small one isn't peeking. Then, quietly as he can, he moves alongside it, pushes up on tiptoes and huffs out into the frosty air, just in front of its broad muzzle. His breath hangs heavily, but he does it a few more times to be sure, then cries out:

'It breathed!'

The little one spins round, eyes wide.

'You did that!'

'Di'n't!'

But he can't keep the grin from his face, and the small one joins him in laughter, relieved.

'Race you to the outside!'

The big one sprints off. The little one races after him, fearful of being left behind.

In summer, the maze is more difficult. The hedges that form it grow tall and dense. But it's easier too. Young couples hand in hand, lazily following sun-dappled paths, pausing in dead ends to exchange a kiss before retracing their steps.

Whole families trying to reach the centre, cheating by boosting the littlest one onto the biggest one's shoulders, spying the statue's horns over the hedge tops and choosing a route accordingly. There's always an ice-cream van up on the hill by the big house and it only takes five minutes to walk there; there are men selling balloons on the lawns out front and people picnicking and children daring each other to jump in the fountains.

In winter, there's nothing. Maybe a lone dog walker skirting the edges, but usually just the crows in the yew trees above, cawing threats at the wood pigeons. Silence, punctuated by those harsh, jarring cries, heart-stopping for a moment before the realisation sets in – it's just a crow. The maze itself is skeletal, and through each hedge corridor the next is visible, so when a squirrel darts along the opposite path, it's a grey streak flashing past the gaps in the hedge. Even the big house seems further away and they don't go up there much when it's cold, cos it's still and silent and all its windows are frosty black like sightless eyes.

They've been coming here so long they know the maze by heart. They used to come with Mum or Grandpa, but now they're allowed to come by themselves as long as they stay together and don't talk to strangers or cross the road without looking both ways, which they solemnly promise each time they leave home. If one of them falls and hurts themselves, they're to run to the man who watches the car park on the other side of the big house, *NOT* run home, because they might get knocked over on the roads and then where would they be?

They reach the maze's edge, exhilarated and rosy-cheeked from their run. Big was imagining he was running to the car park man because Little had fallen and cracked her head on the bench at the maze's centre. Little was imagining she was a unicorn, galloping across the damp grass with rainbows in her mane.

'Where's your mittens?'

'In my pockets.'

The right mitten is retrieved, but the left pocket is patted, examined, turned out, and comes up empty. The little one bites her lip. Mum'll be angry. Mittens cost money. Worse than that, these are her nice mittens, her special not-for-school mittens. They're red but they have silver threads running through them so they glitter. They're her unicorn hooves. She says so to Big, lower lip trembling, and he smiles kindly.

'Don't worry, we'll get it.'

The big one takes the little one's hand and they jog back to the centre, workmanlike this time, navigating with purpose. A turn to the left, ignore the next two turns, then right, then left, then two rights and—

The big one's hand clenches tight.

'Ow!'

The little one wiggles her fingers free, shaking out the pain, affronted. 'Why'd you—'

'Gone.'

And it has. The tree is still there, bare branches dripping melted snow. The bench is still there, wet with drips from the tree above. But statue and mitten are nowhere to be seen.

'We've taken a wrong turn,' says the big one, firmly.

'We didn't.'

'We must've. How else... Did you hear that?'

'What?'

'Laughing.'

'Pigeons.'

'Mmm.'

It didn't really sound like the wood pigeons. It was deeper and nearer. But they had wings. They could fly down into the maze if they wanted. Nothing to stop them doing that.

He won't let himself look too closely at the space where the statue should be. There wouldn't be anything there if he looked, of course, but what if... He pictures two indentations, hoofprints dug deep into the soft ground by heavy stone feet. That statue had been here *years*, maybe even since before the maze. Imagine the imprints it would leave! But that's all it is. Imagining. They've just found a different clearing, that's all. Maybe he should check the ground, just to be sure...

The little one catches movement from the corner of her eye and turns quickly. She thinks she sees a shape disappearing round the corner, but it's partially obscured by the spindly bare twigs, like trying to see through net curtains, so she can't be sure.

'What was that?'

'Nothing.'

'Then why'd you spin round like that?'

'I dunno – squirrel?' She reaches for the big one's hand. She's not sure why she lied. She feels like if she told Big what it looked like, he'd either laugh at her or be scared. She doesn't want either of those things, so she stays quiet. The laugh probably wasn't a pigeon, she knows that, even though she's only little.

Without really discussing it they've emerged from the maze again. An old man with a walking stick and a Labrador nods at them in greeting as he passes. Suddenly the fear and the doubt seem ridiculous. They just got turned round and ended up in a disused clearing. That's all.

And the laughing – it must have been the man. It sounded like a man's laughter, now she thinks about it, deep and rumbly, like Grandpa, or Santa. Sound travels through the maze easily when it's all winter-spindly, that's all. A cool breeze carries the crows' cawing down to her as if to prove her point. The wisps of hair escaping her woolly hat stir in the rush of air and she shivers. That seals it for the big one.

'I'm getting that glove – wait here.'

'No!' the little one shouts, loud enough to attract the attention of the man and his dog.

'Fine, come on then!'

Again they run back to the centre, ignoring all the false paths, concentrating only on the one they know to be correct, the one they know leads to the bench and the tree and the Minotaur statue. A turn to the left, ignore the next two turns, then right, then left, then two rights and—

The big one skids to a stop. The Minotaur is there. The glove is there. The steaming breath is there. Big and Little look at one another. The mitten is on the Minotaur's right horn, the way lost gloves are often placed on railings for safekeeping. The steaming breath is there. The Minotaur isn't moving, frozen to the spot like always, cold eyes unseeing, but there's that breath, that warm breath, curling round its nostrils like smoke from Grandpa's Christmas cigar, hanging near its mouth like words unspoken.

Big stands on tiptoe and reaches for the glove.

SHORTY

Mrs Wickham checks her hair in the bus window. It's silver. She used to get it coloured every six weeks, but she's learned to love her natural shade. It makes coordinating her outfits much easier. When she had Trenchant Mauve she ended up buying a new skirt suit because nothing matched it. Silver is timeless. Silver goes with everything.

Mrs Wickham's dog, Shorty, sits on her lap, safely tucked into the carrying bag. He has a crimson bow in his hair that matches Mrs Wickham's crimson mohair sweater. Mohair hides Shorty's long, silky hair when he moults, which is all the time. The carrying bag, which Mrs Wickham's daughter Evie bought one Christmas, says Louis Vuitton, but it isn't. Shorty doesn't mind. The bag is dark brown to match Shorty's face. Mrs Wickham's loafers are soft fawn, to match Shorty.

Mrs Wickham watches the landscape roll past the bus window, gradually changing from greys to greens. Traffic lights and Belisha beacons become rustic telegraph poles and silver birches. Silver like her hair. She pats it. It's still in place.

She's learned to wash and set it herself. She used to go to the hairdresser every time it needed doing, but she realised it was more for the company than anything else, and Shorty takes care of that now. A couple of afternoons a week she washes her hair in the kitchen sink, then binds it tightly with little plastic rollers that hurt her scalp, and Shorty whines because she isn't giving him her undivided attention.

She thinks Shorty is a pedigree Pekingese, but she can't be sure, because he just showed up on her doorstep. He's not been with Mrs Wickham all that long, but he sure loves his mummy, does Shorty.

'You sure love your mummy, don't you, Shorty?' Mrs Wickham asks. Shorty doesn't answer, but the plume of his tail whisks against the inside of the 'Louis Vuitton' bag.

*

The bus doors shush closed and the driver waves as he pulls away. They're like that, the drivers out here. Friendly. Or maybe Mrs Wickham knows him. She can't be too sure these days. Losing her marbles, Otis says. Spending too much time rattling round the bungalow, Evie says.

'Well, what else am I supposed to do?' Mrs Wickham asks, lifting Shorty out of his bag. Her wrist almost brushes the red bow, but Shorty growls to remind her. Mustn't touch Shorty's bow. Mrs Wickham stoops and fluffs out his tail instead. His fur's matted because he's never been to the salon. Mrs Wickham tried grooming him herself once, but he made such a fuss. Wouldn't sit still in the kitchen sink, and when she tried to towel him dry he went into a huff. She has to make do with trying to brush him when he's sleeping, but then he opens one eye and stares at her. That's when she puts the brush down. You don't want to get on Shorty's bad side.

'Don't want to get on your bad side, do we, Shorty?' He's watching the road. She wonders where he got the bow. Did she buy it, or did he have it already? Perhaps she is getting scatty in her old age.

Mrs Wickham jiggles Shorty's shiny red lead to get his attention.

'Come along, then, Shorty.'

*

Mrs Wickham remembers these streets and misses them. The cobbles were a pain in winter, but Bobby always drove the four-by-four, so it was never too much of a problem, until that business with the brakes. The four-by-four was bottle green to match Bobby's favourite flat cap. Mrs Wickham tried to get him wellingtons that matched too, but Hunter don't make them that shade. It's a good job Shorty didn't show up until after Bobby had gone.

'Bobby would've hated you,' Mrs Wickham tells Shorty. He's straining at his harness and snorting like a piglet. It's not as if he knows where he's going. He's never been here before, and Mrs Wickham couldn't find a decent map to show him.

They pass the vicarage and a pheasant flies up out of the holly bush in the front garden. Shorty threatens it at the top of his voice. Mrs Wickham laughs.

'Oh, Shorty, you're so protective of me. It's just a silly pheasant.'

As they reach the lychgate she suddenly realises why her children wanted to meet her in the churchyard. She suddenly realises why it had to be today. She doesn't have any flowers and feels ashamed. The village post office doesn't sell flowers and you can't get to the farm shop without a car.

'Oh, Shorty,' she says. 'I forgot flowers. I forgot what day it was.'

Shorty doesn't know what day it is either. The significance is lost on him.

*

Evie and Otis are at the graveside with Chris. They're all dressed as if they're going to a garden party, which makes Mrs Wickham feel better about her own outfit. Maybe the date isn't what she thought after all. Maybe it isn't Bobby's... anniversary.

Evie is linking arms with Chris. She's wearing turquoise high heels – Louboutin. They match her turquoise earrings and clash with her bright red lipstick. Mrs Wickham is sure that shade is Chanel. No knock-off brands when Evie's buying for herself. Otis has taken his jacket off even though it's chilly. Probably to show off his shirt, which is covered in a garish pop-art print. Mrs Wickham doesn't like those modern designers. 'Bling,' Otis used to say as a child. 'I like my bling, Mummy.' Bobby gave him a clip round the ear for that. Maybe that was why...

'Ugh, Mummy, where'd you get that?' Evie wrinkles her nose at Shorty. He cocks his leg on a neighbouring gravestone.

'He keeps me company in the bungalow,' says Mrs Wickham, shrugging.

'Well,' Chris butts straight in as usual. 'If you'd reconsider—'

'I don't believe you're acquainted with Shorty.' She tugs Shorty away from the pile of damp leaves he's investigating. 'Shorty, this is Chris. Evie's husband. A lawyer.'

She keeps her eyes on Shorty, but she knows Evie's giving Otis and Chris a look. A look that says, 'See? Old bat's off her rocker!'

Shorty snuffles his flat black nose along Chris's Grenson brogues, leaving a glistening wet streak. Chris steps back, curling his top lip in disgust.

'Homes are different these days, Mummy,' Otis says gently, touching Chris's arm to indicate that he's got this. 'They'll treat you like a queen.'

'And this is Otis,' Mrs Wickham tells Shorty. 'He wanted a dog when he was little, but now he says they're too much responsibility.' Shorty looks up at Otis, then looks to Mrs Wickham for guidance.

'Mummy,' says Evie, trying to step forward, but finding her heel embedded in the soft grass. 'It's obviously not good for you being in the bungalow all alone. We want to take care of you—'

'This is Evie,' says Mrs Wickham. 'She forgets I'm not all alone in the bungalow. I have you to take care of me, don't I, Shorty?'

Anyone else would probably have been stunned into silence at that, but Mrs Wickham's children have expensive educations that prepared them to be masters of any situation. From an early age they were groomed to do whatever it took to come out on top. To step on the hopes and dreams of others if needed. Hopes, dreams, brakes – it's all the same to them. Mrs Wickham supposes she played her part in that, but at least she's finally putting it right.

They all close in on her, pleading with her to give up Shorty, to give up the bungalow, to move into the home, to be quiet and low cost like a good old lady. Mrs Wickham wonders how she raised such monsters. Shorty is still looking up at her, his powder-puff ears slightly lifted as he awaits further instruction. Sad that it has had to come to this, Mrs Wickham nods and lets go of his lead.

'Wonderful, Mummy!' Evie cries, clasping her hands beneath her chin like when she saw Niagara Falls for the first time as a girl. 'It's for your own good, it really is.'

Shorty trots over to Evie and nuzzles her leg like a cat.

'I know.'

Shorty's bow catches on Evie's sheer tights and makes a tiny tear, but Evie doesn't notice; she's too busy beaming at Chris and Otis.

'I know a great estate agent,' Chris says. 'We can handle all that for you.'

Shorty's bow rubs against the bare patch he's made on Evie's ankle.

'Maybe I could take this little fellow in,' says Otis, crouching down. Shorty goes to him and nuzzles his outstretched hand, butting against it with his head, almost knocking the bow astray.

Mrs Wickham wonders if she's made the wrong decision. Otis seems—

'Evie, are you okay?!'

Evie has dropped to the ground. Her teeth are clenched, white froth escaping the corners of her mouth, foaming onto her bright red lips.

'Oh, goodness,' says Mrs Wickham, wondering if her silver hair looks like that against her red sweater when she wears it. A most unbecoming combination.

As Chris crouches beside his wife, frantically thumbing 999 into his huge colour-screen mobile phone, Shorty nudges him for attention. Always seeking attention at the most inopportune—

Otis goes down too. Eyes rolled back in his head, purplish-green veins standing out in his neck, fists clenched.

'Oh my,' says Mrs Wickham. The veins in his neck clash with the print on his shirt. That's why classics like silver are best. The silver *does* look good with the red – Mrs Wickham's sure of it.

Chris pushes Shorty away with the flat of his hand, sending Shorty's bow spinning off into the long grass. He's yelling at the 999 operator as if all this is her fault. Perhaps if he'd listen to her advice rather than being so—

The screen of Chris's expensive Japanese phone breaks as his fist clenches with sudden, involuntary force. Evie is now still, skin taut and pale. Otis's convulsions have subsided to a gentle shuddering. Chris gasps for air. Mrs Wickham picks up his mobile phone. It still works, even with the shattered screen.

'Goes to show, you get what you pay for, Shorty,' Mrs Wickham says, before speaking to the 999 operator.

*

The paramedics eventually leave, clambering back into their ambulance empty-handed. The police take over, cordoning the area off, loading the corpses into the coroner's refrigerated estate car. Shorty has been standing fixed to the spot for a long time, nose to the chilly earth.

'All right, Mrs Wickham,' says the police officer, pocketing his notebook and rubbing his hands together for warmth. 'We'll let you know once we have all the autopsy results, but from what you and the paramedics have said, it looks like some kind of bizarre suicide pact.'

'Goodness,' says Mrs Wickham. 'I had no idea Bobby's death had hit them all so hard. I'm the widow, after all.'

'Well,' says the police officer, breathing into his cupped hands, 'Christmas is approaching. Difficult time for those who've lost someone.' He suddenly seems to realise who he's saying this to and looks awkward. 'Can one of my officers give you a lift? You're quite out of the way here.'

'Oh, no thank you, Officer,' says Mrs Wickham. 'My little Shorty gets carsick.' She hurries over to Shorty before the policeman can protest. No matter how she tugs on the lead, he won't leave whatever he's found. She stoops, parting the blades of grass. The bow. She reaches for it, but Shorty growls.

'All right, all right.' She takes a tissue from her bag, wraps the bow in it carefully and pockets it. Shorty wags his tail.

'Happy now?' asks Mrs Wickham, holding the lychgate open and waiting for him to waddle through.

'So long as they don't put me in the hold for the flight,' says Shorty.

'Oh no, Shorty,' says Mrs Wickham, patting his head. 'You'll be on my lap on the plane. Assistance dogs get special permissions.'

That's the thing about Shorty. You don't want to get on his bad side.

DEAD MEN DON'T COUNT

'It don't count as stealing if they're dead!' Crom tells you for the millionth time. Like he's trying to convince himself he ain't a thief. He hangs back even though the dead man's penned in. You've already done your part – dragging over an old oak cabinet, a heavy farmhouse table and a low cupboard filled with pots and pans to keep the dead man from interfering with Crom's work.

The man's a few years dead. Little more than a skeleton clad in strips of foul-smelling, discoloured flesh, he bumps against the cabinet, rattling the blue and white china inside. Little of his eyes remain, and yet you feel he's looking at you with a deep sadness, judging you, your actions, your life choices. As if there was any choice about it.

Crom gives the makeshift holding pen a wide berth. It makes no difference to the dead man. He continues bumping against the cabinet, will do so until he rots away entirely or one of the Registry comes and finishes him off.

Once he's safely past, Crom pokes out his tongue and waggles it at the dead man, as if he's outwitted him somehow.

You hate Crom sometimes. His easy acceptance of everything the Home and the Registry tell him. Sure, he's young, but still old enough to have a mind of his own. He notices you giving him a look, and says, 'Everyone knows if they bite you, you get it.'

You roll your eyes. 'They only bite when people are mean to them. Which is all the time.'

You've never seen one of them attack unprovoked. Never ever. When the Registry shot Mama, she was just going to stroke your hair. You knew it, because it's what she always used to do, and that's what the dead do. They get stuck in loops and repeat the actions they carried out when they were alive, over and over. Like a bit of them remembers somehow. Mama was going to stroke your hair, not claw your face like the Registry man said.

'You'd be the expert,' Crom mutters under his breath, and you want to knock the smart words out of his mouth, but he's got work to do.

In the far corner of the room there's a safe. It's big and old, the kind that needs careful, precise movements, like mending a pocket watch. You can't just explode these with dynamite like the new ones. They're sturdy and fragile at the same time. Some kind of moron, Dada called it, but you can't remember the proper word.

You think of Dada's big strong hands, the hands that made your breakfast every morning and packed your satchel for school, even after the bad times, even after there was no school and his hands was just bones. Dangerous, the Registry men said. Mama and Dada weren't no danger to no one, least of all men with guns.

Crom has set down his bag of tools and is carefully laying them out. You leave him to it. If he's so keen to rob this old man, let him do it alone. You wander back to the man's pen and idly poke through the drawers in the bottom half of the cabinet.

Mostly it's been picked clean already. There's just a couple of books and a dusty old box of photos. You drag the photos out and thumb through them, trying to find one of the dead man when he was alive.

'What are you doing?' Crom calls to you. He's on his knees in front of the safe, turning the dial with his ear close to it, trying to determine the contact area. 'Stop shuffling paper around. I need to hear this!'

You doubt it's the photos affecting his concentration. It's the dead man. Crom is terrified of them. He saw some film when he was a toddler, too young to understand it was make-believe, some made-up thing about dead men who just wanted to eat people's brains, so he has it in his head that's how they actually *are*. His parents were took away as soon as they got ill, so he never saw what they was actually like after. He just has all these pictures in his head of them being like the movie dead men. 'Zombers', he calls them. Silly name for a silly idea. Even the Home don't let you call them that. Though they don't like you calling them people neither.

Your flicking fingers land on a photo. The man's wearing the same coat he has on now. It ain't all rotted and dusty, but it's definitely the same, with wide silky lapels and brass buttons. His eyes were blue when he had them, and he looks friendly in a sad sort of way, same as now, really. There are more pictures: him playing with a little girl, him holding a fluffy little dog on his knee, him fiddling with some machine back when there was 'lectricity.

You realise suddenly that the only sound is the *click click click* of Crom spinning the dial to park the wheels. The dead man has stopped bumping and he's watching you. Well, not watching, cos he don't have eyes, but regarding you in that way they have.

It makes you smile, and you ache for Mama and Dada. They was good parents, even after. Even the Registry lady was surprised. Expected a feral child, she said, not to find you all washed and brushed and well fed. She said it like maybe, just maybe, the Registry man shouldn't have shot them. Even though just hinting that's treason. If the Registry man wasn't shaking so bad, he might've turned her in after handing you over to the Home.

You've leaned over the pen and given the box to him without even thinking about it and he's taken it in his bony hands. He clacks his jaw like he's thanking you, but everyone says that's silly, like thinking dogs have personalities. There's a chair in there with him and he sits down on it and puts the box on his knee and rifles through the photos, holding each one at arm's length for a moment like he's looking at them.

'He ain't looking at them, you know,' says Crom.

You wonder how long you've been watching the dead man, because Crom's all done and he has the tools back in the bag and the bag on his shoulder and all he's got out the safe is a little black box.

'What is it?' you ask, nodding to the box.

'He ain't looking at them, cos he ain't got eyes or a heart or a mind.'

You take the box from Crom's unresisting hands and open it up. There's two rings inside, both silver, both engraved with the same date, a date just before you were born.

'They just pretends to be alive so they can trick ya,' Crom tells you sagely. 'That's when they goes for your brains.'

The dead man has stopped on one photo. He's been holding it for the longest time. Eventually he lets it slip from his skeletal fingers and it drops to the dusty flagstone floor. He slumps forward in his seat like a man defeated. You crane your neck to see the photo, while Crom tugs on your sleeve.

'Leave him, leave him for the Registry,' he complains. 'We should get back to the Home.'

'In a minute.' You dismiss him with a wave of your hand. The photo is of the dead man, younger, not much older'n you, and with him there's another man with dark curls and they're clutching hands and gazing into each other's eyes and they're both wearing dove-grey suits and brooches of flowers and happy smiles.

You wipe your eyes quickly and you know Crom's seen, but for once he don't rag you about it; he just swallows and puts the rings in his pocket.

'They was as happy as Mama and Dada,' you say, your voice high and childish.

'I know,' says Crom, patting your arm. 'I know.'

GRANDMA'S FEAST DAY

Tomorrow would be Grandma's feast day. The first in a while, which was both good and bad, Esther thought as she carefully combed Grandma's thin hair over the kitchen sink. Twisting it up into a clip, she snipped the topknot off with big scissors and tossed it into her hair box with the few others that hadn't already been spun into thread or used to stuff pillows. Next, she took the clip out again and lathered Grandma's whole head with soap. She could have used the electric shaver, she supposed, but it seemed wasteful when a razor would do the job just as well.

There were still a few stubby candles left from Grandpa's feast day, and as the sun dipped lower, she lit them to illuminate her work. As it grew darker still, Renee came in, eyes red and puffy from crying. Esther found it strange that feast days still hit her little sister so hard. Renee had grown up knowing nothing else. Esther remembered the mass funerals, when death was a time of public mourning, rather than a celebration of a life well lived.

No one wore black to a feast day. They wore the dead's favourite colour, or an outfit the deceased had complimented, or, if they were of an age and size, the dead's own favourite outfit. Grandma was all high-waisted trousers and thin polyester sweaters. Esther doubted anyone would be coming to feast in those.

'You found anything?' Esther asked. Renee sat down on the cool tiles of the kitchen floor, skinny legs drawn up, pointed chin on her knees. She reached into her pocket and took out a motherboard and an adapter cable with the plug missing.

'Might be able to match the cable to a plug,' she said, wiping her running nose on the back of her hand.

'And the motherboard? What good are those anymore?'

'Man at the market collects them.'

Esther rolled her eyes. Probably some pipe dream of going back to how things were. Renee begrudged working at the best of times, was useless when she was sad or preoccupied. Esther largely preferred life now, in spite of everything. Everyone got along, because they had to. People shared. Helped one another. And Esther and Renee had a pony, a fat little Shetland called Arthur who hauled heavy scrap when they needed him to and sometimes gave them rides and the rest of the time munched his way through all the thorny plants and scrub growing outside the shack, producing bags and bags of fertiliser for the village crops. Kids like Esther and Renee could never have had a pony *before*.

'Why don't you help me?' asked Esther, drawing the razor in careful lines across Grandma's head and swishing the fine grey hairs loose in a large metal bowl of soapy water.

Renee's eyes widened and she looked horrified.

'Not like that!' said Esther quickly. 'Just boil some water and put together the herb poultice.'

Fresh tears sprang to Renee's eyes, but she complied.

'It'll be a broth,' said Esther quietly. 'I requested it specially. You won't have to carve, or anything.' Renee bit her quivering lip and remained silent.

Esther finished up Grandma's head and gently towelled it dry; she kissed the smooth dome of cold flesh. Afterwards, she used the small scissors to clean under Grandma's nails. Some preppers didn't do that, and it wasn't strictly necessary, but Esther took pride in the small details. She hoped someone would show her the same respect when her time came. Not all villages were so civilised as theirs.

There was a soft knock at the door, a formality which suggested it was an old person. Everyone knew everything about everyone – what was the point in locks and knocks?

'Come in!'

Mrs Partridge did so, hesitantly. She was wearing Grandma's old polyester sweater, the red one, and cream high-waisted trousers, darkened with mud. Her hands were muddy too. She wiped them ineffectually on her thighs. 'Me and the boys are done with the pit. You let us know when she's ready to go in and we'll help carry her over.'

Renee let out a little whimper and scurried off to her room.

'She still finding it hard, huh?'

'Yeah.' Esther scrunched up a twist of cotton torn from Dad's shirt and dipped it into the barely warmed pan of water. Shook her head at its lukewarmth and put it aside until the water was hotter. 'Easier than Mum and Dad's of course, and she's at least old enough to understand why, now, but...'

'It's a shame she hasn't taken to it,' Mrs Partridge admitted. 'But I'm sure she'll get into the swing of things once the feast starts. One of the boys found a string for Sherwin's guitar, so we'll have music again, and Becky made some silk flowers from her mum's wedding dress so we can reuse them every time now.'

'That's nice.' Esther smiled. 'Any vegetables?'

Mrs Partridge looked away. 'Alex found a bramble bush. There were a few ripe berries. He's taken a cutting, and marked it, so next time—'

'Fruit!' Esther hugged herself. 'Oh, it's so long since I had fruit!'

'Don't get too excited, there's only a handful. I'm sure you and Renee will get one though, what with being the bereaved and all.'

Esther nodded. The village was generous – they'd likely vote for Renee and Esther to take on distribution of the berries themselves.

'Anyway,' – Mrs Partridge turned to go – 'like I said, give us a shout when you're ready.' Esther nodded. The water was steaming now.

'I won't be much longer.'

*

The following morning, Esther awoke in a foul mood. Renee had hidden in her room all night to avoid helping, so Esther'd had to load Arthur up with the deadwood and kindling and lead him, and without her direct involvement in carrying Grandma, Mrs Partridge's 'boys' were careless and clumsy and ripped the foil she'd spent the best part of an hour wrapping. So then they had to bumble around in the dark trying to find suitable leaves and God knows if what they used to patch the hole in the foil was edible, because all greens looked the same by twilight.

The sun had almost risen again by the time Esther got to bed, and Renee got up not long after and set about grooming Arthur. Every time Esther started to doze off, there it was, the scrape of the curry comb. Her fists squeezed tighter and tighter with each scrape until eventually her nails hurt the palms of her hands and she had to get up.

'What are you doing?' she asked, hands on hips like Mum used to stand – not that Renee would remember.

'I've been thinking,' said Renee, not even looking up from Arthur's mane, which she was untangling with her fingers. Typical that she'd switched to a silent job now. 'Maybe we could start a new tradition.'

Esther could tell she wasn't going to like whatever Renee was about to suggest, but she waited for her sister to spit it out.

'I was thinking' – she fluffed Arthur's forelock, stalling – 'we could eat Arthur. Instead.'

'Arthur!' Esther was horrified. She couldn't believe her own flesh and blood could be so wasteful and stupid. 'Arthur's alive!'

'I know, I know, but Mr Partridge used to be a butcher, so...'

'And who will tow scrap and haul water then? Where will we get fertiliser for the vegetable patch or Alex's cuttings? Did you think about that? No, because you're too selfish!'

'The vegetable patch is dead,' Renee said flatly, moving on before Esther could offer a rebuttal. 'Mrs Partridge's sons could do the hauling. They're strong. Arthur's not going to be hauling scrap forever, anyway. He'll have his own feast day if the winter's cold enough.' Renee burst into tears again, so Esther spoke more gently than her sister deserved.

'Exactly. When it's his time. Now it's Grandma's time.' That just induced even louder sobs. Desperate not to wake the whole village prematurely, Esther blurted: 'Becky said that Michael told her he saw wild ponies on the fen. So when Arthur's feast day comes, we'll go and catch another, the whole village together, and we'll tame it and—'

'I hope it's feral and furious and it kicks you in the head and you die!' Renee almost screamed before sprinting off towards the treeline, braids flying.

'If I do I'll make sure they roast me and use me as a centrepiece with an apple in my mouth!' Esther screamed back.

The wall of the neighbouring shack creaked and Esther was sure it was because Becky was trying to see through the gaps in the siding. Bloody nosy cow.

*

The broth smelled like roast beef, although Esther supposed that was just down to the copious amounts of rosemary Mrs Partridge had used. Daylight was fading. Michael and Oscar fetched candles from their uncle and Sherwin busied himself putting up the mosquito nets while the youngest played with Alyssa's tame fox under the table. It still brought back the occasional rabbit from the woods, but they'd been getting smaller and runtier as time went on.

Esther glanced again at the treeline. It'd be just like her fool sister to trip on a tree root and break her neck and let herself spoil out there in the woods until she was no good to anyone. They'd have to start soon. It was already a terrible waste of wood keeping the pot warm. Another winter like the last and they'd need all the log reserves they had.

'Shall I?' asked Mrs Partridge, ladle poised over the cooking pot.

'Please do,' said Esther, holding out her bowl.

They'd got all the way round to Alex before Renee finally took up her seat. She looked tired and pinched and angry. She hadn't even changed her clothes, still in outgrown jeans and a stained vest rather than the florals Grandma loved so much. When Mrs Partridge offered the ladle to her, Renee shook her head. Thin gravy dripped onto the chipped ceramic plate. Mrs Partridge looked to Esther for guidance.

'Please, Renee,' Esther begged. She'd feared something like this. There were no carrots or potatoes anymore – couldn't Renee get that into her skull? But Renee shook her head again and turned her plate over emphatically. Esther sighed and Mrs Partridge shrugged and moved on to Sherwin.

All throughout dinner, Esther watched her sister, feeling worse and worse with every mouthful. Renee was the only one left. The only member of their family not gone to feast. Uncle Tony had been first and Renee was so little she'd snatched the crackling straight off the serving plate before Aunt Sylvie got her helping, but everyone had just laughed and laughed and passed the minted peas and the unleavened bread. Then Mum and Sylvie both together in that incident with the neighbouring village. Thank goodness those bad old days were over. Then Grandpa, and then Dad, and now Grandma, and Esther and Renee were the only ones left.

Renee picked at Becky's silk flowers with her stubby fingernails, giving them her full attention. Her eyes were red-rimmed and prominent in her gaunt face. Esther hated to see her that way. Why couldn't that damned useless fox have caught a rabbit? Or the boys could have fished in the river. They hadn't been out since Alex reckoned he saw that scout from the other village, but Esther was certain that was foolish nonsense. Alex was scared of his own shadow. If she knew how to fish Esther could do it herself. Perhaps if they didn't need a prepper for a while, she'd learn.

She wiped her bowl clean with a plantain leaf and then folded it in on itself and tossed it into her mouth. Renee continued to fiddle with the silk flowers, looking at no one, speaking to no one. The anger had drained out of her. She just looked blank – an expression all too familiar to Esther.

Alex brought out the berries in a fancy turquoise bowl, china thin as paper. He seemed to take personal pride in the precious fruit, which was understandable. It wasn't the kind of thing you found every day. The berries were like jewels, a perfect, glistening, purple-black handful of precious gems. Around the table everyone was smiling, oohing and ahhing over them like they were a newborn baby. Some of the younger ones licked their lips. The older ones were less obvious, but the eagerness was in their eyes too. The desire to pop the soft fruit against the rooves of their mouths, feel the rich, sweet juice squirt to the back of their throats. They were savouring the taste before it had even passed their lips.

Esther picked up the bowl, and held it close against her chest as she turned Renee's plate back over. Cradled the precious fruits carefully between her breasts as she wiped the drop of gravy away with her sleeve. They were all still smiling. They all still thought she was just giving Renee the first one, as would be proper, as anyone would, as was expected.

As she upended the turquoise bowl and watched all the berries tumble out onto her sister's plate, she could hear their shocked gasps all around her, the scrape of a few chairs as some feasters left in disgust, Becky saying: 'She can't *do* that! She *can't*!' And cutting through all of it, another sound, a sound as rare and perfect as those berries.

Renee's delighted laughter.

The only sound that mattered.

BLANKS

Day One

'Who is your Original?' asks the doctor, shining a bright light in your eyes. You blink, glancing left and right. Either side of you are others, blank, damp and hairless like you. Doctors take their temperatures, their blood, their heart rates.

'I...' Your tongue feels thick and clumsy in your mouth, like you've never used it before.

'Who is your Original?' he asks again, lowering his flashlight and peering intensely into your face instead. You feel ashamed for some reason, aware of your paper gown and scrawny forearms. You avert your eyes and shake your head, taking furtive glances in his direction to see his response.

He nods and gestures to the door, already looking towards the next one in line. You try to rise, but your legs shiver and give out and you go sprawling. The doctor sighs and waves over an orderly with a wheelchair. He scoops you in, gently but without compassion, and wheels you out into the corridor.

There are more hairless people out here, but their appearance is slightly more varied. Different skin tones and heights and builds, although all are lean. What little muscle they have lacks definition. All have that strange, waxy look to their skin, like they could use a good soak to melt away the top layer and be fresh and clean underneath.

'Can you get in the chair by yourself?' the orderly asks and you nod, dragging yourself across. He disappears back into the other room with the wheelchair.

You study the palms of your hands. Your fingertips are wrinkled as if you've spent a long time submerged in water, but you can't shake the feeling that you need to scrub your skin clean.

'This is a travesty,' says the person alongside you. They have a long face, smooth skin, high brows and round cheeks. They are better at speaking than you, seem generally stronger and more together than you. You can only look at them helplessly.

The person tenderly takes your hand, and you are certain this is the first skin-to-skin contact you've ever felt.

'Did the Education not take?' they ask you gently. 'Can you understand me at all?'

'I...' you manage, then nod, hoping this person will get your meaning.

'Talking difficult?' they say, and you nod again, grateful this time. 'Don't worry. It's different for everyone. I'm quick to adapt, I guess.'

A nurse comes over with a clipboard, pulls off two sheets and hands one to each of you.

'You can switch with the others if you want. Switch as many times as you like, but once you sign the bottom, that's you.'

The sheet is some kind of registration form. It's full of someone's details, their name, their address, their national insurance number. This sheet says Aja Sawyer. The person next to you has a sheet that says Wren Aster.

'I think I'm more of an Aja, don't you?' says the person.

You shrug. You're unsure what any of this means.

The person takes the sheet from your unresisting hands and gives you theirs.

'Now I'm Aja,' they say, 'and you're Wren. Do you like that, or should I try to trade it for you?'

'Wren?' you ask. At least you can say that.

'Yes,' says Aja. 'That's us now, I guess. Wren and Aja. Understand?'

You nod. You're being named. Assigned an identity at a time when you can't possibly know if it's you or not. Wren's okay, you suppose.

The nurse returns with two Ziploc bags filled with folded yellow fabric. You and Aja are given one each. Aja throws off their paper gown and takes the yellow overalls out of the bag, stepping into them one leg at a time, like everybody else.

'What are you, shy?' asks the nurse with a smirk. You realise that you are. You also realise that it's silly. Aja's body is smooth and genderless all the way down and you know yours will be too. It still feels weird, but Aja and the nurse are looking at you expectantly so you wriggle out of the gown, still sitting, and then struggle into the overalls, accepting every bit of help Aja offers.

Day Ten

'You sure you don't want me to pick up a wig for you?' asks Aja, checking this latest one in the mirror. It's long and ash blonde with a chunky fringe. You shake your head. It's easier for Aja. Aja knows she is female. She may not have the breasts and hips of her Original, but she's positive that her Original was female and she is too. She's not permitted to look into it, of course. No Blank will ever know their Original; that's the law. You're not sure whether the Originals get to know their Blanks. That part's not stressed every five minutes on the Info Channel.

You don't think it'd matter to Aja if she found her Original anyway. He could be a seventeen-stone rugby player with cauliflower ears and a smile like a busted piano, and Aja would still be Aja. She would still apply her fake lashes each day and look longingly at dresses in the online catalogues. She would still slip lip glosses into the sleeves of her overalls when the chemist's security guard was otherwise occupied. Even though theft, any crime, carries 'serious consequences' for a Blank, because their very existence is a privilege.

Your very existence.

A privilege.

The little cement block you and Aja share, just big enough for your sleeping sacks and the info screen, that's a privilege. The colourless, odourless, tasteless, but nutritionally balanced noodles you're fed for every meal, they are a privilege. The Education you receive each day via headphones while you stitch yellow overalls and seal sleeping sacks into Ziploc bags, that's a privilege. So are the steam showers that clean you after each day's productivity; so too is the chain-link fence round the enclave keeping the protestors out. You're not really sure what privilege means, or protestors, or what they are protesting. Perhaps you'll learn it in tomorrow's Education.

Day Twelve

They're just people. Protesters are actual people, not Blanks. They're holding printed signs and their clothes are all different, like you heard about from Aja. She says it's early days yet, and someday soon, Blanks won't have to wear the yellow overalls: they'll be able to wear whatever they want. You ask if she means like real people and she narrows her eyes and says, 'We're real,' all angry, and you apologise automatically without knowing what got her so riled.

These people seem riled too. You get a little closer, trying to read their signs. Your reading is coming along, but it's hard. You don't pick things up quickly like Aja. She's flying through a book the chemist's security guard gave her, and she doesn't even move her lips when she reads it.

One of them spits at you. The globule of saliva hits your thigh, soaking in, warm and wet. You look from it to the man who did it and back again. They're so hairy, people. He has a beard and a hairy neck and huge savage eyebrows. Even Aja's crossest face doesn't look so cross as that.

'Freak!' he shouts. 'Abomination!'

Others take up the chant, favouring 'freak' over the longer word. They press against the chain-link fence and it bows towards you alarmingly, yet you can't tear yourself away. One of these could be your Original. Your Original has hair and eyebrows and maybe even a penis or a vagina. It's a funny thought. You can't imagine it. The biological stuff in your Education, your first Education – the one with all the weird visuals – is still very clear in your mind.

The yelling reaches a crescendo and you realise one of them has you by the collar of your overalls. She's a woman, middle-aged, but strong. She has her foot braced against the fence and seems intent on pulling you through it, even though the gaps are far too small. But as she holds you close, the cold metal links bite into your skin, and the protesters surge forward, tearing at your clothes, scratching at your hands and face.

You're reminded of the blood tests, but this is prolonged and worsening and you can't help but cry out. Everything happens very quickly then. A shot disperses them, and Aja is there with the chemist's security guard and they disentangle you from the fence and carry you between them to the med hangar. You keep glancing back, and they think that it's to see the crowd and tell you not to, but really it's to see if you left any bits of you behind, any scraps of skin flapping on the fence, because it feels like some of you is missing.

Day ??

You're warm. It's an unusual feeling. Normally, even when you snuggle close to Aja, the concrete is cold and the thin sleeping sack does little. But here you are warm, and the air smells of something, something rich and sweet. You lift your head, look down at your forearms. They are covered in soft downy hair. You try to stroke it, but you're weak. Your breath gurgles in your throat.

You become aware of the tube then, and you panic, gagging. Your lungs feel soggy and heavy, struggling to draw in air. You gasp and cry and Bonnie hurries into the room.

Day Twelve (Later)

'Mother!' You sit up, choking.

Aja and the chemist's security guard are standing over you.

Aja looks confused. The security guard looks perturbed. He pulls Aja away from your bedside and they whisper to each other.

You check your arms. Smooth as ever. No hair, no tube in your throat, no crushing moisture in your lungs, no sweet-rich smell.

And no mother.

Day Twenty

Aja is shaking you awake. The info screen hasn't lit up yet – it isn't time to work. You prop yourself onto your elbows and look at her. You can't sit up any higher in the concrete confines of your block, and neither can she. It's not time for the shutter to unlock yet. You say so to Aja.

'I know, but I can open it.' She slips a small metal rod out of her sleeve, not much larger than one of her tubes of lip gloss. She puts it in the corner of the shutter.

'The shutter's for our safety,' you tell Aja, frightened. 'We shouldn't leave the block without a human escort.'

'We'll have an escort.' She presses her thumb into an indentation in the top of the rod and a light comes out of it, like a laser pointer, only hot. You can feel the heat from here.

'Is this about my dreams?' you ask.

'They're not dreams,' says Aja, grimacing. Perhaps the rod is uncomfortably warm to hold. It looks like it could be. Eventually the shutter clicks, beeps three times and then slides open. The cold dawn air rushes in and you shiver.

Outside, everything looks grey, even your skin. Aja reaches back inside the block and pulls down the sleeping sacks, her spare wig and her book. There's nothing more to take. Everything else is in the communal areas of the complex. Blanks aren't really supposed to own anything.

'Not dreams?' you say. The chemist's security guard is waiting. His name is Rick – you know that now. He looks sick with worry. His chin is stubbled and his eyes are bloodshot.

Aja shushes you. You are the same biological age and yet she always makes you feel like a child. Although you suppose it's justified. You did wander up to the fence and get scratched by protestors. Which meant you had to spend some time in the infirmary. Which meant Rick had to make up a lie about how you got there so you didn't get mulched. Mulching is what happens to disobedient Blanks. It's something to do with reclaiming genetic material. You're not sure of the specifics. Rick looked sick when you asked about it, even sicker than he looks now.

Rick's van is parked by the gate, big and black.

'Cameras are off,' he tells Aja. 'We've got maybe five minutes before they notice, tops.' He hands her a sheaf of paper held together with a bulldog clip. 'If I stop the van again once we're through the gate, just get out and run. And whatever you do, don't lose these.'

Aja nods, and as he helps her up into the back of the van, they hold each other's hands a little longer than necessary. You look away, hoping it'll give them room to kiss goodbye, but they don't. He lifts you in and closes the van doors.

'Where are we going?' you ask.

'Put these on,' says Aja, pushing a cardboard box towards you. There's a pile of musty old clothes inside, in varying sizes. As the van pulls away, you try to choose between dungarees that smell of sweat and a pair of leggings imbued with stale farts.

Day Twenty-Five

You're living among the people now, so you get to wear people clothes all the time. It's not so great. You can't afford good ones anyway. You're staying in an abandoned church with Herve and Manny, two old homeless guys. They both have big unkempt beards. You wish you could grow a beard. They look like they would keep your face warm. You ask Herve about it and he scratches and tells you it's a time-saver, but that's about it.

Aja has spent the last few days going to and from the newspaper office. The first day you didn't go with her, because Manny found a tiny kitten mewling in the graveyard's undergrowth and you helped him feed it with milk from an old syringe. Now she won't let you go, because she says people might recognise you. Apparently, your Original is some big deal. She says she's seen photos of them, but she won't even tell you if they're a boy or a girl.

'You're too impressionable,' she explains one night, as the four of you huddle round a fire Herve started in a weird big gold pot shaped like an eagle. 'Like a little baby goose. If you saw them, you'd start trying to be like them.'

'So? I am them.'

'No. You're you.'

She doesn't get cross anymore, she just looks tired.

'Don't know how I'd feel about a load of other mes walking about doing their own thing,' says Herve, thoughtfully. 'But I got no money anyway, so it's not something I'd ever have to worry about.'

'Money?' you ask.

'Sure,' says Manny, stroking the kitten still nestled in his coat. 'Didn't you know you guys were expensive?'

Day ??

There's a tree, a tall glittering tree like you've never seen before, and you're sitting under it. Your hands are pudgy and marked with felt-tip pen. Your artwork is above the mantelpiece. You've drawn a big reindeer with a red nose, pulling a huge sleigh stacked high with presents.

You're sitting cross-legged, holding on to your ankles, and you're so excited that you're worried you might pee. You're rocking back and forth slightly to help keep that from happening. Your mum has gone out to the garage and she's bringing you your main present and you already have a bike, so...

The living room door opens and the puppy races in. She jumps all over you, licking your face, her tail wagging. She's a labradoodle with fuzzy black fur and a wide pink grin. You yell to your mum that she's wonderful and her name is Lily and you have to go and pee now so you don't have an accident.

Day Twenty-Seven

You awake to the sound of Manny crying in the vestibule. Herve is with him, has his arm round him and is whispering soft, reassuring sounds. You get up and tiptoe over to them. Better not wake Aja. She needs her beauty sleep, she's always saying.

'Kitten's dead,' says Herve flatly.

Manny's holding it in his big hairy hands, trying to massage life back into the tiny, limp body, grey and white and cold like pawprints in snow.

'We should give him a proper burial,' you say. 'My mum used to do it with my little pets, before I got Lily.'

'You guys don't have mums,' says Herve, frowning. Manny's only half listening, but he sniffles and nods.

'What can we put him in?' he asks.

Day Twenty-Eight

You thought you'd seen Aja mad before, but it turns out you hadn't. Right now she's yelling in your face. Then she strides away, kicks over the big gold eagle pot, sending the ashes from last night's fire spilling everywhere, hops around holding her toes and swearing fit to bust. You're crying, but you don't really know why. You realise now that the box and the papers you shredded to give the kitten a comfy coffin to sleep in forever, that box and those papers were Aja's. Or yours. Or the complex's. Point is, they were important and official and now they're all shredded up and buried out in the graveyard between the human plots.

Aja is crouching down now, still holding her foot, but she's stopped shouting and instead she's crying, huge wracking sobs with snot and tears that'll wreck her perfect make-up. Manny goes over and awkwardly tries to put an arm round her. She shrugs him off at first, then changes her mind and buries her face in his dirty overcoat, adding to its layer of filth with her tears and her snot and her runny make-up. Manny doesn't seem to mind, though. He just strokes her hair and tells her we'll work something out.

She shakes her head.

'It's over now. Press man needs proof, and we don't have any anymore.'

'Y'still got Wren,' says Herve.

Everyone goes quiet then, and there's just the sound of you and Aja sniffing in tandem.

Day Twenty-Nine

It's strange being out in the world. This place is busier than any you've seen. You know from your Education that it's a city. Sort of like the complex, only bigger and the people can go wherever they want, whenever they want. You're in a big shiny office building, sitting in their big shiny reception.

Aja has you all dressed up like a wazzock. You learned that word from Herve. Anyone vaguely silly is a daft wazzock in Herve's eyes. Politicians. Manny. You. But it's never been truer than now. Aja's put you in a long blonde wig, a big floppy hat and oversized sunglasses. She bought your things from a charity shop. There's a shapeless pale lemon dress and lots of bangles and a horrible fur scarf thing made from a dead fox. Aja says people will focus on how crazy you're dressed and not bother to look at your face.

The receptionist certainly looked at you for a long time. You wonder if you should have dressed all smart like Aja, because the receptionist barely gave her a second glance. She looks immaculate as usual in a skirt suit and high heels and a new wig, jet black with a streak of white in the fringe. You're pretty sure she got them the same way she used to get her lip glosses and it worries you because if mulching was a risk at the complex, then that risk is doubled out here. Blanks aren't even supposed to be mixing with people.

A man approaches and Aja drops the magazine she was nervously leafing through and stands up, smoothing her skirt.

'Is this…?' asks the man, nodding at you. 'She doesn't look—'

'They,' says Aja firmly.

'Sorry,' says the man, looking like he means it. 'Sorry, I should've thought. Come with me.'

He leads you down a corridor lined with image boards and you recognise some of the people in them from the Info Channel. Human celebrities. Singers and chefs and actors and musicians. The Info Channel said you could never be like them, because Blanks don't have souls and you need a soul to sing or cook or act or play an instrument. You tried singing once, on your own in the steam room, and you could, so you guess Aja's right about the Info Channel telling lies.

He leads you into a room, and it's large for just the three of you, with a big long table and six comfy leather chairs. He sits on the far side of the table and you and Aja sit opposite. There's a comms box in the centre of the table and you look at it and imagine being important enough to take calls on it.

'So,' says the man, after he's introduced himself as Simon Trent and shaken hands with you. He doesn't say anything more, but Aja seems to understand, because she gently removes your oversized sunglasses from your face, folds them carefully and tucks them away in her shoulder bag. She takes your hat and your wig next, both together, and then unwinds the horrid old fox scarf from round your neck. Simon Trent gawps at you the whole time.

'Wow,' he says. 'The likeness is uncanny.'

Aja rolls her eyes. 'Of course it is. What did you expect?'

Simon Trent blushes. 'Yeah, yeah, I know, but... It's not like we get to see you guys often. Cloistered away in the compound—'

'Complex.'

'Right.'

Aja and Simon talk for a while and your mind wanders. You think about your dreams, the shiny tree and Lily the dog. They seemed so real. You can smell that front room, the fresh piney scent of the tree, cooking smells drifting from the kitchen, and Lily's distinctive earthy odour. You remember her sitting in front of the fire, tongue lolling, dripping onto the carpet like a freshly cooked rasher of bacon. Bacon. You've never even had bacon.

The comms box beeps and Simon presses an indentation on its glossy black surface. The receptionist's voice comes through, as clear as if she were in the room. You look round to make sure she isn't.

'Ms Donovan is on the phone,' she says, sounding almost frightened. 'She knows.'

'Oh.' Simon doesn't look frightened, just tired. His shoulders sag. He glances at you and then at Aja. 'I guess that's made our decision for us. Tell her we'll arrange a meeting.'

There's an intake of breath like the receptionist wants to say something else, but Simon presses the indentation again and cuts her off.

'What?' asks Aja, her voice icy. 'You think we're just going to go over there?'

Simon's eyes are sad, like Manny when he thinks about the kitten, only not so wet.

'She's got resources like you wouldn't believe,' he says, rubbing the surface of the comms box with his sleeve like it's dirty, although you can't see any dirt. 'If she knows... they're here, it's only a matter of time before she tracks them down.'

Aja's fury is different this time, all cold and tight, like she doesn't quite know what to do with it.

'You realise this could be as good as mulching them?'

He looks pained at that, closes his eyes, shakes his head. 'No, no, surely not. She wouldn't—'

'Why do you think she made us?' Aja says every word very clearly, like she used to speak to you when you first woke up, only not so kind.

Day Thirty

Aja keeps apologising to you. Won't stop, even though you've said it's fine. You don't even know what she's so sorry about. She has hardly eaten or slept since you got back from the press office. Herve and Manny were on at her to sit down, to eat something, but she just kept pacing the church and went crazy every time you tried to go outside.

Now you're on the doorstep of some big house and Manny and Herve and Aja and Simon stayed at the bottom of the drive, outside the tall electric gates, and it feels like the first day of school. That was another one of your dreams, and not as nice as the others. You were wearing a blazer a few sizes too big and all hot and itchy, and another bigger girl pulled your pigtails and said you were stuck-up or something like that.

Aja let you choose your own clothes today, so you have wide calf-length shorts and a bright orange V-neck sweater. No wig, just the sun on your scalp, although Herve made you wear his hat for the walk there in case anyone realised you were a Blank.

A light breeze tickles your calves and you wonder about activating the entry system, but the voice from the electric gate said someone would be down in a moment. They are, and it's a broad-shouldered lady who looks a little like Aja, but Aja if she'd lived her whole life on steak and chips and cakes instead of nutritionally balanced noodles. And of course she's hairy like they all are.

She ushers you inside and you can't take your eyes off the downy hairs surrounding her shiny peach-painted lips. The house has that smell, that warm, rich smell from your dreams, and you notice the woman's arms and apron are dusted with flour and you realise she's been baking. That's the smell, those melt-in-the-mouth flapjacks she makes, this woman, Bonnie.

The hallway is dominated by a huge, broad staircase with a sweeping banister rail and a carpet the colour of one of Aja's lip glosses. Dusky Rose or Evening Petunia, something like that. A quavering voice calls down from upstairs: 'Bonnie! Is that her, Bonnie?'

The woman looks you up and down, her thick, dark brows drawing together.

'I think so. You want her up there?'

'Of course!'

There's a big bed in the middle of the room. It's surrounded by strange bags of liquid and tubes making sucking and shushing noises and machines with flashing lights on them. You stand and stare at them until Bonnie pushes you nearer to the bed, and then you see her. You feel mean flinching at a person, but you can't help it. She looks like you, but thin – so, so thin; it hurts you to look at her spindly arms. They're stuck through with tubes, clear liquid going in and brownish-red liquid going out. She has eyelashes and they're gummed together so her eyes are just crusted slits, but they're the same colour as yours, the exact same. She smiles weakly at you and you don't know what to do.

'Bring us some tea, please, Bonnie,' says the spindly woman in the bed, before breaking into a coughing fit, wet and wracking. Aja warned you about this. Not to eat or drink anything they offer in case it's drugged. Herve said something about waking up in a bathtub of ice, although in this summer heat, you think that might not be so bad. Then you remember what Aja said next, sounding sadder and angrier than ever: 'That's for people, Herve. Blanks don't get to wake up at all.'

You shake your head to protest against tea, but Bonnie's already bustled out of the room, and the spindly woman's staring at you with those crusted-up eyes.

'So,' she says, just like Simon, only you don't have Aja here and you don't know what's expected of you. You don't have any layers to take off this time, so you just sit down awkwardly in the silky, frilly armchair by the side of the bed.

The machines make a whole lot of competing noises. Sucking and shushing, beeping and blipping. You watch lights flash and liquids make their way along tubes, wondering what they are and where they're going to. You're no longer sure which ones are going in and which ones are going out, so you occupy yourself trying to trace them to their source.

Bonnie returns with a tray and a teapot with swirling gold and pink patterns all over it and little matching china cups. The tea is fragrant and you can't imagine drugs would smell like that, but you still shake your head and tuck your hands into your lap so you're not tempted to take a cup. Bonnie gives you a long look, but the spindly lady just laughs and waves her away.

'It's not what you think,' she says. 'I understand why you'd be frightened, but...' Coughing overtakes her again, and you reach out, wanting to comfort her somehow, because you know how that coughing feels, you've been there and done it. 'I never realised,' she says when the coughing eases, and her eyes are still dry but there are tears in her voice. 'I never thought that you'd be people. I'm sorry – I'm so sorry.' Her voice is wet, like she's speaking through swamp water. It makes you want to clear your throat in sympathy. 'I harvested so many of you trying to buy a few more years, a few more months, a few more days. And you know what? Some of the technicians at the complex raised concerns. Unexpected brainwaves. Impossible REM sleep indicators. And I ignored them. Even though I felt you, even though I dreamed your dreams. I put it down to coincidence, the illness, the drugs. I just wanted to live – can you understand that?'

'Of course,' you say. 'Everyone wants to live. And even if they don't, other people want them to.'

And then she cries and cries and tells you everything and you struggle to follow, and Bonnie comes in and strokes the lady's hair and tells her to calm herself.

Day Fifty-One

You miss the lady. She laughed every time you called her that, begged you to call her Alex, or at least Ms Donovan, but you couldn't, because that would mean accepting she was separate from you, and you didn't want that. Whatever weird quirk linked the two of you, you didn't want it ever to be severed, not even after she died.

It wasn't a one-way thing – you know that now. She felt you, just like you felt her. She realised the Blanks weren't blank at all and that's why she woke them, started the Education and the complex, stopped making new ones. But as she saw that world through your eyes, through your dreams, she realised it wasn't enough. She wanted you all to have lives, real lives, the lives you deserved. She didn't want Blanks to be judged for her actions, or the actions of their Originals. But people are slow to react, even slower to learn than you. She complained every day about red tape, ranted to Bonnie about how she'd come up with the damn technique, why couldn't she be the one to end it? And hurry as she might, she ran out of time.

And now she's dead and it's worse than the kitten, worse even than Lily. Bonnie stands by you at the graveside. You're wearing a black dress and a tie and brogues even though Aja said you couldn't wear things like that together. You watch them cover the lady's beautiful box with soil and hope that Lily and the kitten will find her and play with her, even though they were buried miles away. It's down to you now to get everything finished. A big responsibility for one small Blank.

Simon's at the funeral too, and lots of other press men, and they take a thousand pictures of you, their cameras flashing over and over until you feel you'll go blind. An old, old woman comes up to you and squeezes your hand, smiling at you. Aja opens her mouth, looking worried, like she wants to stop what's about to happen, but you recognise the old woman and hurry past Aja. When the old woman speaks, you finally know that the lady was right, that everything will be okay.

'Alex told me about the arrangement,' the old woman says, in a voice that once dictated the number of biscuits you could have, a voice that defined bedtime and soothed boo-boos. 'I thought she was crazy at first, but now I've seen you, I understand.'

Yes, different but the same, you think, smiling at your mother. Just like all the other Blanks. Just like everyone.

MRS SUTHERLAND'S ARMS

'...And you'll need to take these.' Mum balances tins on top of the folded fleecy blankets piled in my arms. 'And this.' She adds a flask. 'Put that in a bowl for her and fetch cutlery. Help her eat if needs be.'

'Aww, Mum!' I protest, but she's pulling her coat on over her scrubs and hasn't got time for my complaints, wouldn't hang around to listen even if she did.

'Take Lexi with you,' she continues, pointing at my little sister like I won't know who she means. 'She can feed Davey while you get the genny back up and running.'

'Awwww, Muuuuuuuuuuummmmm!' Feeding Davey is the best part – the only good part – of checking on Mrs Sutherland. Lexi ruins everything. And Mrs Sutherland is creepy, what with all her stumps and her watery eyes. Never been in her basement but that's where her generator will be, because it's where ours is and all these old houses are built the same. Bound to be even creepier than she is. But I know there's no point complaining about any of that, because for whatever reason Mum feels like we gotta look after Mrs Sutherland and Mum'll just find a way of making me feel bad if I go on about it. Talking about how Mrs Sutherland's family don't speak to her anymore and all her friends are dead and blah blah blah.

'And deadbolt everything before you go,' Mum says as she's at the door. 'Y'hear me? Everything. Don't want anyone getting in, do we?'

I shake my head and the movement makes the flask roll so I have to jam my chin down to stop it falling to the floor. It's Mum's chicken soup and it's like liquid gold in wintertime. She does dumplings with it, but Mrs Sutherland's not getting any of those, because me and Lexi gobbled them all up. The dumplings are the best part, the very best part of Mum's chicken soup.

'Okay then, be good, Scally,' and she tries to ruffle my hair, but I've parted it and waxed it down so hard it's going nowhere. Military-style.

She locks the door behind her even though me and Lexi are going out in five minutes, because you can't leave the door unlocked, not even for five seconds, not in our neighbourhood. 'Specially while Dad's away.

It ends up taking longer than five minutes anyway. Lexi has to wear her wellie boots because of the snow, and if she's wearing her wellie boots then she has to wear her tights too because her socks rub otherwise, but she doesn't want her tights on and I have to pin her to the bed and wrestle them on her while she kicks and screams. She's too big for this. I wasn't behaving like that at her age, I'm sure of it. Then she wants to wear her stupid glittery fairy wings, but she can't wear them under her coat, because it would gape open and it's too cold for that, so I have to spend ten minutes wriggling the straps over the layers of jumper and jacket and coat on her little sausage arms. Finally I zip her up, and she looks up at me with trails of snot running down her top lip like the gross little gremlin she is and I tell her to wipe it off on her gloves. Bad idea, because then she wants to hold my hand.

Fortunately, I've got the blankets and the cans and the flask to carry, so I couldn't really hold her hand even if I wanted to, and she has to content herself with her fairy wand. Getting to Mrs Sutherland's takes longer than expected too, even though it's literally across the road, because Lexi insists on poking her wand into the snow at every step and wiggling it around. She does it and does it and does it and just when I'm about to scream at her to pack it in, she stabs a dog turd hidden beneath the crisp white crust and bursts into tears because her pretty sparkly wand is ruined.

'Hey,' I say, holding the flask in place with my face again. 'Just rub it in the clean snow and we can wash it at Mrs Sutherland's. She won't mind.'

'In the snow?' Lexi sobs. 'In the snow?! There might be more poo in the snow!'

'Not if you do it by Mrs Sutherland's door. No other dogs would do it there, would they? Davey'd scare them away!'

At the mention of Davey her face brightens and she nods. Tears freeze on her cheeks and eyelashes, making them glittery as her wand. She cleans it as best she can while I speak to Mrs Sutherland's security system. It's super sophisticated and I always wonder why she lives round here if she can afford tech like that. She should be in a mansion or something, with assistance robots to bring her soup and restart her crappy generator.

The system recognises me from the approved guest list and the electronic locks flash green. I push the door open and usher Lexi in before they can flick red and leave her stranded. The door closes behind us, and Davey rushes up, wagging his tail, a big smile on his broad, dopey face. It's as cold as outside in the hallway, and I put my pile of supplies down on the floor and spend extra time patting his silky back and rubbing his ears to warm my hands. I realise after a few minutes of this that if I can see my breath, Mrs Sutherland can see hers too, and that's not good for an old, old lady, especially one who can't move well.

I tell Lexi to take Davey and the cans into the kitchen, and then I head to the lounge with the blankets and the soup. Mrs Sutherland is watching her television with the volume turned up and the curtains closed. Using her emergency portable genny for her TV instead of her heating. Old person priorities! Her expression's glazed and she has a blanket, but it's that type of knitting that looks like lace and has big frilly holes in it. It's sliding off her shoulders and I can't help but stare at the shiny stumps of her forearms. She doesn't notice me standing there, so I do my best not to freak out. I wrap one of Mum's blankets round her tightly, tucking it under her chin, taking care not to go anywhere near those handless nubs.

She turns to look at me then and gives me a shaky smile. Her eyes are red and droopy like a bloodhound, but the rest of her face is surprisingly young, and her haircut – well, it's cooler than mine. The sides are shaved and her greying hair has been teased into a scruffy mohawk. There's a tattoo on the side of her head, a winged fist that looks pretty familiar but

I'm not sure where from. She sees me staring and reaches up self-consciously with one of those stumps. It takes everything I have not to recoil.

'Was just the way we had to have it,' she explains. 'I got used to it.'

I don't want her to realise how grossed out I am by her lack of hands, so I wave the flask around and say: 'Got some of Mum's soup, want it?'

'Please,' she nods, and I hurry to join Lexi. 'And could you bring me my arms?' she calls over the drone of her game show. I'm sort of relieved. At least that means she'll feed herself.

In the kitchen, Lexi sits cross-legged on the floor, watching Davey try to lick the enamel off his bowl. Her fairy wand is resting in the sink, although she doesn't seem to have made any attempt to wash it.

'You seen Mrs S's arms?' I ask as I pour the soup into a bowl and hover my hand just above it, making sure it's warm, but not too hot.

'I'll find them!' Lexi jumps to her feet and thuds off up the stairs with Davey scampering after her. She's fascinated by Mrs Sutherland's cybernetic arms. Doesn't find them creepy at all. Kids are weird.

I stay in the kitchen as long as I can so I don't have to go through to Mrs Sutherland until she has her arms. I nose through the cupboards, find some crackers and put them on a small plate so Mrs S can crumble them into her soup if she wants. I add Mum's tins to the cupboards. They're already packed with old lady food. Tinned peaches and tinned puddings and weird square tins of reformed meat with little keys to open them. Not sure if those are for Davey or Mrs S.

Finally I hear Davey's paws on the stairs again and then Lexi's boots – a few quick thumps and one extra-big one as she jumps from halfway up the stairs. If she drops Mrs S's arms and breaks them, Mum will go spare, so I hurry out to scold her, but she's already in the front room. I wait awkwardly in the doorway with my tray of soup and crackers as Lexi helps Mrs Sutherland into her arms, carefully lining up the transmitters as if there's nothing gross about it.

'How comes you don't wear them all the time?' she asks. I cringe, but Mrs Sutherland just smiles.

'Well, it'd be like you wearing your wellies all the time. They're good for some things, but not everything.'

'My wellie boots ARE good for everything!' says Lexi indignantly, and Mrs Sutherland laughs and folds her hands in her lap with a whirr of hydraulics.

'Why'd you go with the metallic finish?' I ask, handing her the tray and watching as the titanium digits close round it. 'Synthskin looks more real.'

'If you're all young and smooth and wrinkle-free,' she says with a snort.

I shrug and turn for the door. If I go and do the genny now, I won't have to wipe her chin or help her find her legs or anything like that.

'Looks cooler, don't you think?' I hear her say to Lexi, and Lexi says: 'If ever I have to get one, mine will be rainbow glitter!'

I shake my head and open the basement door, picking up a heavy-duty flashlight from the hallway cabinet. Stupid Lexi. Dad would be furious to hear her say that, I'm sure of it.

If it was cold upstairs, it's freezing down here. My breath fogs the air in front of me, and Davey appears by my side and patters down into the darkness without hesitation. I keep the torchlight trained on his tail as long as I can, but when I reach the bottom of the stairs, he's disappeared. I can still hear him snuffling and panting, though. I leave him to it and make for the generator. It's cold to the touch – must have been off for some hours. I feel a pang of guilt at coming here so grudgingly. Can't be a barrel of laughs for Mrs S, no heat in the dead of winter. Makes more sense why she put the mini-gen on the TV now – it'd only warm one room at a time anyway, so she'd either have to stay put in one spot or lug it round with her. I can just about remember a time when none of us had generators and the power grid was reliable, but that was before Lexi was born, when I had Mum and Dad to myself. Good times all round.

At least the coolness of the generator means I can get straight down to refilling the tank. There's plenty of canisters down here and a nozzle, so I unscrew the nearest one and get to work. Within a few minutes the tank's full, and the generator whirs to life as soon as I punch in the reboot code.

The light flickers on, cobwebs drifting across the bare bulb to create strange misshapen shadows on the bare brick walls. In the centre of the room is a hulking something with a tarpaulin over it. Dunno how I didn't trip over it when I came down. Davey's under the tarpaulin, and I call him to come out, but he won't budge. He's found an interesting scent down there and seems intent on sniffing all the flavour out of it. I don't want to leave without him, so I lift the corner of the tarp and reach for his collar.

Whatever's under there, it's metal and military green and has a tread on it like a tank. Is it a tank? No. It's big, but not that big. And how would she even get something like that down here? I let go of Davey's collar and he bounds back up the stairs, leaving me alone with the whatever it is.

I pull the tarp back a little more. Who's to say how far under I had to crawl to get Davey out? The explanation is already forming, on standby in case I need it later. There's one of the treads on each side, and they're roughly triangular, raising the body of the thing up high. The front is toughened glass, and on either side there are huge jointed pneumatic rods, each with a fixture not a million miles away from the ones on Mrs Sutherland's arms. I stare at the thing for a long time, knowing what it is, but disbelieving.

'Can I have a go in it?' I look down and Lexi's beside me, twiddling her wand between her fingers.

'No,' I say, quickly pulling the tarp back down, trying to make sure it looks exactly as I found it. 'They're not toys. And don't you say nothing to Mrs S.'

She rolls her eyes and skips back upstairs, and I hurry after her but already she's yelling: 'Mrs S, Mrs S, can I have a go in your mech?'

Mrs S is standing up when we get back. She's taller than expected, but it's hard to tell how much of that is down to her legs. I thought she might be cross, but she just looks a little sad. She touches Lexi's shoulder and says: 'Why don't we go take a closer look, huh?' She gives me a long hard stare then, but I'm not sure what it means.

Mrs S clunks down the stairs, her legs hissing and buzzing with each step. She looks tired when we get to the bottom, like it takes more effort to lift those legs than you might think.

'So you lost your arms and legs in the war?' I say, wincing as soon as the words are out of my mouth. I'm as bad as Lexi.

'You could say that.' She pulls the tarpaulin to the ground with a grand sweep. The mech is huge, frightening. Lexi doesn't seem to notice. She swings off one of the arms, pulls herself up into the cockpit as soon as Mrs S opens the hatch.

'How do I make it move? Can I fire the guns? Does it have rockets?'

Mrs Sutherland laughs. 'No! You can't make it move, because you don't have the interface implants. I was bomb disposal, so no rockets. And in any case, it was decommissioned years ago. You think they'd let me keep a weapon that can punch through a tank?'

'So why'd you bring it home?' asks Lexi, instantly bored.

I'm looking at that fist again: it's there, on the mech's paintwork, stencilled in black. A clenched fist with wings either side. And I know where I've seen it before. And I know why Mrs S doesn't have any arms or legs. And my stomach clenches as I imagine Dad in some military hospital, being carved up and fitted for his own mech to take to the front lines. A strangled sob bursts out of my mouth against my wishes and I pound back up the stairs, out of the front door, into the street. And I double over and look at the snow and it makes me dizzy the way the sun catches it and my tears melt little black holes in the white until I see spots everywhere and feel like I'm going to die.

'Sally!' Mrs Sutherland's calling from her doorway and I want to tell her everyone, absolutely everyone calls me Scally, but it isn't true because Dad doesn't and anyway my breath's still tearing through my chest, powering the sobs.

Suddenly Davey has joined me outside and the snow makes him crazy. He runs in tight circles round me with his back humped up like a horseshoe and before I know it I'm laughing at him and forgetting... forgetting that my dad is probably... that when he gets home he'll be... I straighten my back, laughter gone, tears dried up, nothing left but me.

I look up at Mrs S and she holds her hand out to me. Lexi is at her side, peeping out round the floral old-lady dress. Her little pudgy fingers grip Mrs S's other hand tight, like it isn't so bad to touch. I move forward, my own fingers outstretched towards that robot hand. If Lexi can do it, I can do it too, because the best thing about me, the absolute best thing, is I'm the oldest, bravest one.

A WINTER CROSSING

There were cannibal rats on Rathburn. Or so the legend went.

Roger's eyes had widened at the story and Carrie immediately regretted telling it. She was regretting it all the more now.

As the binoculars were dutifully placed in her outstretched hand, she glanced at Roger. The lad was chewing a piece of loose skin from the edge of his fingernail and looking from the sea to Carrie and back again with large, worried eyes. Sighing, she raised the binoculars.

The waves looked like crumpled tinfoil, silvered peaks throwing up the grey light of the dying sun. Something bobbed in the distance, something pinkish and vaguely spherical.

'You talking about that buoy over there?'

'It wasn't a buoy!'

'Fine.' Carrie tossed the binoculars back to her crewmate. 'It was a severed head. Want to take the rowboat out and investigate?'

'Forget it.' He turned away from the railings. 'Tea?'

She nodded her approval and while Roger disappeared below decks, Carrie leaned on the railings and looked out to the bleak white horizon.

Cannibal rats might be pushing it, but in winter Rathburn wasn't much of a holiday destination, that was for sure. Once-sunny beaches turned to bleak stretches of slate, winds howling around the ruined castle. The castle where all the rat bones were found. In the legend.

During these long, cold months, MS *Rosenberg*'s job was to load up with food and supplies for the few resident islanders eking out a remote existence. Islanders like Roger's family, who ran the only tavern and arranged accommodation for summer visitors. Carrie shook her head. How could an island boy get so rattled by a few silly stories? Carrie loved that island and she hadn't even grown up there.

'Captain Roberts?' Roger's voice was muffled, coming from the small kitchen below deck.

Carrie watched a kittiwake bobbing on the waves a few metres away.

'What?'

The seabird rode the neaps, ducking its head under the water every few moments, sometimes coming up with a small silver fish dangling from its beak, sometimes with nothing.

'Where did you put everything?'

A dark shape, probably a seal, appeared beneath the kittiwake and circled slowly just below the surface.

'What everything? I didn't put anything anywhere!'

'The tea, the coffee, the bread, the tins – it's all gone!' Roger's voice rose, getting louder and more panicked with every word. Carrie could picture him crashing about in the galley like a deranged cow, slamming the cupboards and throwing the contents all over.

'Hell's teeth!' Carrie headed for the stairs, her back to the kittiwake, which finally noticed its circling admirer and peered down into the water. It withdrew its head abruptly, letting out a loud squawk and flapping its wings to make a hasty getaway.

Carrie joined Roger in the galley and found him half buried in the cupboard under the sink, digging around in the bucket of cleaning products.

'You're not going to find tea in there, are you?'

Roger scuttled backwards and slammed the door shut, getting to his feet.

'Someone else is on board.'

'Yes, Roger, there's Moss.'

'Apart from you, me and Moss!' Roger snapped.

Carrie softened. Roger seldom had a harsh word for anyone.

'Maybe Moss forgot to restock,' she said gently, patting Roger's shoulder. 'Let's go and ask him.'

Moss and Carrie had worked the *Rosenberg* together for thirty years. If anyone had forgotten to restock the kitchen, it was Roger, but Carrie wasn't about to go pointing the finger right now. They'd be docking at Rathburn in an hour, for crying out loud, they could all cope without tea and biscuits for that long.

Propelling Roger forward, her hand still on the lad's shoulder, Carrie headed back to the small navigation room at the front of the ship.

'Moss, would y—' The words died on her lips. Moss wasn't there. His fluorescent jacket lay on the floor beside the ship's control panel. The autopilot was engaged, but in these unpredictable winter seas, Moss liked to keep an eye on things in case the human touch was needed.

'Probably stepped out to pee,' Carrie said with more certainty than she felt. She finally let go of Roger and nudged Moss's jacket with her toe. His walkie-talkie lay on top of it. As she stooped to pick it up, there was a loud yell and a splash from the deck.

'Moss!'

Roger was out the door so quickly Carrie's bones ached at the mere thought of moving at such speed.

'He's gone,' said Roger quietly as Carrie joined him on deck.

'Don't be ridiculous, Roger – damn fool probably fell in pissing over the side.' Although the odds of an old seadog like Moss overbalancing on a day as still as this were close to zero.

At least, it had been still. Now, the water churned, like Moss was thrashing just below the surface, but couldn't break through. It made sense – he was a strong swimmer, but the water was cold, freezing. The shock of it would make it a trial to do anything other than splash. Even if he wasn't wearing a life jacket, it wasn't as if he'd just sink like a stone.

'I'll get the rowboat. He'll freeze to death in there.'

'I'll go,' Roger offered.

'No, no,' Carrie waved him away, already unlashing the boat from where it was stowed. 'You get on the radio and contact the coastguard.'

Carrie heard Roger's sharp intake of breath and turned towards him. He was shaking, head darting left and right like a startled animal.

'Saw something!'

'What?'

'Something just leaped onto the boat! I saw it!'

'Roger.' Carrie put a little of the old sea captain into her voice. 'Stop scaring yourself and contact the coastguard.'

'No,' said Roger. 'There's something on the boat. It was big and dark green. I saw it!'

He stepped past Carrie and snatched the rowboat, yanking it down onto the deck with a strength born of fear. He pulled his life jacket tighter, lowered the boat over the edge and clambered down after it.

'I'll get Moss,' he called up. 'You get rid of that *thing* and call the coastguard!'

'There is no *thing*!' Carrie yelled after him, her temper finally getting the better of her.

And then she saw it. Not in the boat, but in the water, a dark shape lurking alongside Roger's oars.

'Roger,' she called down, although the young man was already pulling away, his long, practised strokes fighting the roiling water. 'Mind out – there's a seal near you. Watch he doesn't capsize you!'

Roger stopped rowing for a moment, cupped a hand to his ear to show he hadn't heard. Carrie was about to repeat herself when she noticed a thick fog had rolled in all around them, deadening all sound. The sea, seconds ago a boiling froth of motion, was now like a sheet of glass. The kind of silence you hear when something gets stuck in your throat. Long seconds where you can't breathe and the world stops.

A splash broke the silence, and things moved so fast Carrie couldn't take in what happened. The seal leaped clear of the water, crashing into the rowboat; Roger yelled; the wood of the rowboat cracked and Roger disappeared beneath the surface.

Carrie gripped the railings, staring into the water, rooted to the spot. Roger should have surfaced by now. He was wearing a life jacket – if the cold overwhelmed him and he couldn't paddle, he should bob to the top like a buoy. Seals weren't usually aggressive outside breeding season, just misguidedly playful. Even if it had dragged him beneath the surface, it would've let go by now.

She hurried to the radio to call the coastguard, trying to slow down what had happened, to replay it, but it was all too fast. A couple of ideas nagged at her, though. The 'thing' – she hated to call it that – was too long and lean to be a seal. It moved more like a dolphin, arcing through the water, but its dark green scaled hide ruled that out—

Carrie stopped dead in the control room doorway. The radio was smashed and smoking, wires and circuit boards exposed. Its casing was cracked as if someone had hit it with an axe. Moss's coat still lay on the floor, but now it was wet. There was water everywhere, all over the floor, dripping off the radio.

Radio.

Carrie stooped and felt around in Moss's jacket. The walkie-talkie was still there. She exhaled slowly.

Not far to Rathburn. Just change the frequency on this thing and contact the lighthouse.

Carrie focused on the walkie-talkie. It was the new model Roger had insisted they get, even though the old one worked perfectly fine. The old one just had one dial to turn and a single large button to press. This one had an LCD screen with a pallid green glow and an entire keypad of numbers and symbols she couldn't see properly without her reading glasses. Every time she pushed the transmit button, the radio merely crackled and hissed. Goddammit – Roger had got this just so he could seem useful, and then right when she needed him to help her with it, he had to go and—

The blow hit her full in the back and she could do little to stop her face smacking against the deck with a loud crack. Her first thought was pirates, although even as she thought it, it struck her as odd that they'd bother with the *Rosenberg*. Stealing a rusty motor ship didn't seem right.

And then, after she'd been pinned a few seconds, there was sniffing close to her neck and the stench of rotting seaweed. Bile rose in her throat and without thinking she jerked an elbow loose and jabbed her attacker in the ribs. The thing – and thing did not seem like such a foolish word anymore – issued a sound. It was an echoing, alien shriek. Carrie was up and running before she'd even thought about it, ignoring the throb of her arthritic joints.

Out on the deck she looked back. Through swimming vision and teary eyes from the blow to her head, she made out a dark humanoid shape, a glint of teeth and claws. All the encouragement she needed to dive from the prow and swim desperately towards the floating remnants of the rowboat with long, jagged strokes.

Gasping for breath, expecting needle teeth to clamp round her leg any second, her shaking fingers closed round a plank of driftwood and she let her chin drop onto the solid surface.

*

She came round when the cold bit into her bones. She wasn't sure how long she'd been out; she strained to lift her head, craned her neck for a landmark.

And there it was, portside, the craggy lump of Rathburn Island. She was almost into the bay. If she could make—

Something moved on Rathburn Hill, a flash of midnight green. She closed her eyes. Cormorants, glossy feathers reflecting the green of the ocean below. Nothing more.

Unbidden, the old name for Rathburn popped into her head. Ratbone. The story she'd told Roger a lifetime ago: a colony of rats had swum to the island from a sinking ship in the 1800s. With no natural predators, the rats thrived and the colony grew and grew until—

Shaking her head, Carrie fought down the growing dread that she'd forever be trapped between the things in the sea and the things on the island. She kicked out, using her waning strength to power towards the bay.

The tide was coming in and aided her journey, although the current was washing her towards the cave set into the side of Rathburn Hill. She didn't want to go in there, but lacked the strength to steer back towards the rocky beach. Nearing the cave mouth, she saw them. Dark shapes perched in every nook. As the darkness swallowed her, she closed her eyes and longed to reach the other side. Cormorants? Creatures? No, it was just her mind playing tricks on her, making a monster of every shape and shadow. Although when she reached the island proper? Now that's a different story.

So the legend goes.

SOMETHING OR NOTHING

You can tell when you're closing in on a runner because of the dogs. Mary always liked dogs, but you have to be careful with them these days. Some still wear collars, a remnant of their past lives, but their eyes are haunted and hungry, and no one's going to be calling 'walkies' to them any time soon. The rain doesn't seem to bother them, though, not when there's a runner to be followed. A big Alsatian cross has his nose to the ground, trying to smell his way through the damp to the fleeing soldier. Mary watches him carefully and when he lopes off again, she leads the troop in the same direction. She still hasn't figured out why the dogs are so interested in runners. Perhaps they sense the fear and it makes them think an easy meal is on the way. They should know by now nothing is easy.

The rain keeps coming. It infiltrates. Down their shirt collars, behind the straps of their webbing, dripping into their eyes from the rims of their helmets. The sky is grey and the fields are brown. Churned by the tread of the tanks and the mechs that have gone before, water pooling in the furrows and the irrigation channels running between the fields. This used to be a desert place. Then they dropped one of those lightning rods, and it sent its purple pulses up into the sky and the rains came and never stopped. The irrigation ditches went from important to pointless in a matter of days.

Rolls is the one who spots him. The runner. Her fist goes up and everyone behind comes to a halt, rifles clanging against body armour. She points. His skin's mottled, violent orange and purple and green. His hair's slicked to his face, eyes shut, mouth open, lying back in the ditch as the water level creeps up his legs, soaking into his trousers, closer to his bare torso and gaping mouth with each raindrop. There's a dog in front of him, some wet black spaniel thing, its coat hanging in sodden ringlets beneath its belly. It makes to sniff the man's face, but the Alsatian bares his fangs and the smaller dog backs off. It's then that the troop gets a clear view of the man's shoulder, and they know they've all seen it, because there's a collective rigidity to the group that wasn't there before, an intake of breath like they're one lung forgetting how to exhale. Everyone worries it could be them. That they're one Grey ambush, one Eater onslaught from running like this poor coward.

Apart from Sister Mary. She shoos the dogs away, walks straight up to him and squats down like it's nothing. It's important that they think that. If it becomes something it's too easy for them to go to pieces. That's why she allows the nickname, ludicrous as it is. She's no one's sister. Their Big Guys made sure of that. And she never worked on a ward, and her time in the convent wasn't what everyone makes it out to be. But if they think it, well, that's what it is.

'Someone find his arm,' Mary barks, and they all look at each other, drawing straws with their eyes before Rolls and Rabbie move off, dipping their toes into the deeper ditches, trying to turn up the missing limb. Soon they're distant figures, tiny as Greys. Mary's inspecting the ragged stump. 'Torn,' she says, more to herself than to the rookies behind her, who have gone decidedly green around the gills. 'Probably one of their Big Guys.'

'What good's his arm going to do him?' It's that new one, straight off the shuttle and every bit as useless as you might expect.

'One less thing for their damn Eaters to clean up,' Mary says, cupping the runner's cold face in her hands. Why the Eaters don't eat the dogs is another mystery. The Big Guys are a different story, pulverising anything that gets within reach, but the dogs are probably smart enough to stay out of range. Maybe they just give the Eaters a wide berth too.

'Coward,' the new one spits at the fallen man. Mary ignores him.

'Hey,' she says to the runner, 'Takahashi? You in there, kid?'

She feels the squad encircling her, watching. One of them scratches the spaniel's neck absentmindedly and is lucky to get only a wagging tail in response. Rookies lose fingers that way. Whole hands if infection sets in.

Mary presses Takahashi's face tighter. The blood's still dripping from his shoulder stump, but she doesn't bother with a tourniquet, not yet. Waste of resources while the other thing's inside him. He jerks, and two of the rookies leap back, one slipping and sprawling into the mud. The others are too nervous to laugh, but the dogs scatter, barking and growling.

Mary blocks the commotion out, focusing all her attention on Corporal Takahashi. His eyes open, but they're rolled back in his head. His lips part and a low groan escapes.

'He's alive!' one of them says and presses a button in their helmet, ready to request an evac. Rolls comes in over the comms and overrides the command. Seconds later, she's there in person, Rabbie at her side.

'Not yet,' she says, and she's holding Takahashi's severed arm in two hands, carrying it by the wrist and bicep like a second rifle. Her own rifle hangs by her waist. Rabbie's hand is on his trigger, not twitchy, just ready. He is focused fully on the perimeter, mindful of Husks, his eyes bright and watchful as the dogs'.

Everyone else's eyes are on Sister Mary. Even Corporal Takahashi's, although she knows he doesn't see her, not yet. Something does, though. She straddles him, and his forehead dips back into the dank water of the channel like she's baptising him, but she's not, she's doing something far more invasive, and the thing in there knows it and it starts speaking through Takahashi's mouth, first in its language: *Kroka um ai amaki*, then in theirs: *You would seek to reduce one who has transcended?*

Transcended. They dress it up in the words they've learned and there are factions of humans who believe them. It's not transcendence, it's a slow death, a fate worse than the Eaters. It's a parasite that gradually consumes its host. There's a reason the squaddies nicknamed them Husks. Squaddies and their nicknames. Eaters, Greys, Big Guys. And she goes along with it, because there's power in the naming of things. Letting some things stay unnamed – that's powerful too.

She used to get self-conscious about this part, embarrassed even, talking to them in front of her squadmates, but now she's done it enough times to know rookies tend to hear whatever they want to hear rather than what she actually says. 'You fuck off,' she tells it. 'You fuck off out of him.'

This shell is dying, it whispers. *You can't save it, but I can.*

'Brave words for someone hiding out alone in a flood zone in a one-armed man. You think you're going to get more like this?'

They always come. It sounds almost smug, but she can feel its grip slipping. They don't like to be engaged; they like you to be cowed and quivering, awed by their power. They don't know what to do with questions.

'Rabbie, get the medispray out my belt,' she says, and feels it surge under her hands as he does so.

Yes. You serve me.

'No,' she assures it. 'Now, fuck OFF!' and she gives Takahashi a final squeeze and puts her everything into it, squeezes his face so hard her gloved fingertips tear the water-softened flesh. The dogs all begin howling as one and it hates this, Mary can feel that, it hates the dogs more than anything. The hairs are standing up on her arms. It's putting up a fight, but there's nowhere else for it to go. Everyone here is too strong. Afraid, but not in the right way to give it an opening. There's a sound like a pulse rifle discharging and a flash of golden light, although Mary has never dared ask whether anyone else sees and hears those. His back arches and then relaxes, and the livid orange drains from his skin, leaving only the mottling of a near corpse. The dogs fall silent. Gradually they peel away, loping off back to wherever they shelter. All except the black spaniel.

The Alsatian keeps looking back over its shoulder, but it seems the spaniel's mind is made up.

Mary works fast then, taking the spray can from Rabbie's patiently waiting hand and emptying half of it onto that ragged stump of a shoulder. Rolls makes the evac call, and while they wait for the shuttle she wraps Takahashi in layer upon layer of foil blankets and oversees the rookies clumsily loading him onto the stretcher.

*

When the drop ship arrives, conversation resumes and there's that special kind of jubilance just on the edge of hysteria. She's seen it before. The spaniel hops on board and lies down under the seats and if anyone even notices it, they make no mention of it. Mary's the last one on board, and after she's secured Takahashi, she clips her own safety harness into place only to find that the newbie has engineered his way into the seat beside her. His eyes are big and shining and he leans into her shyly so the others won't hear and says: 'You exorcised it, didn't you, ma'am?'

She looks out of the window, watching the waterlogged countryside recede into nothing. We dress it up in the words we've learned. 'Sure,' she says. 'If you like. Whatever.'

Under her legs, the spaniel's tail thumps the floor.

CLOCKWORK MEN AND
CLOCKWORK DOGS AND FROGS

'Very good, Adriel. Now, if you could set the upper appendage ambulator to... let's say... ten horizontal oscillations per minute. That should give us a nice slow wave.'

As Adriel made the necessary adjustments to the apparatus, Josie leaned forward and examined the scene through the eye of her camera. The count now looked far cheerier and more animated, although little could be done for his slack facial expression. Josie had yet to develop the suitable techniques for enlivening inert facial muscles, but her experiments with mild electrical pulses and Adriel's sleeping visage had proved encouraging. (To her, at least; Adriel was less enthused.)

The sleeping dachshund at the count's feet looked good, but having another in a similar pose just wasn't working. Josie stepped out from behind her camera, stroking her chin thoughtfully, and stared at the little dead dog.

'Adriel, could you retrieve another articulated support frame from the carriage? Infant-size should do.'

Adriel left the room grumbling about dead-thing smell and

the weight of corpses. Josie smiled. For all his complaints, she knew he enjoyed the work. He was learning a lot about photography and was approaching the point where he might be permitted to operate the camera. Not move it or align the plates. That would be too great a responsibility at this stage in his education. But replacing the cap after her careful exposure countdown would make an exciting change for him. He usually just lifted the bodies into the support frames and adjusted their limbs. She might even let him choose a pose for one of them this time. One limb, not the entire body. Wouldn't want to overtax his creativity.

As Josie mused on this, tapping the pleasing solid black box of her camera with a fingertip, one of the countess's maids bustled in with a tea tray. There was a short scream and a clatter of crockery. Josie turned to attend the stricken woman, hoping the jolt of the tray hadn't knocked the camera's focusing plates out of alignment, as it had taken a little over an hour to bring about a pin-sharp image, and she'd rather not go through the whole tiresome process again with Adriel sighing and complaining about how his shoes pinched.

'Oh goodness, madam, I am sorry, madam,' said the maid, her hands fluttering ineffectually over the shards of teacup as Josie gathered them together. 'It was just seeing His Countship—'

'His Honour,' Josie corrected automatically.

'...His Honour up and about again. After his... accident.'

Josie knew her work was good, but 'up and about again' was a bit of a stretch. Still, she was used to friends and family members of the deceased reacting strongly to her work, and not always positively. Necromancidermy, the penny papers had called it. Which was a rather big word for them, if a little confused.

'It's really nothing to be alarmed about,' she said, unable to bring herself to give the maid a comforting pat. She opted for her most soothing tone instead. 'It's purely to give the illusion of life and movement for the photo. A lovely memento for all the family.' She realised she sounded like her own calling card, but was at a loss for anything else to say.

Fortunately, Adriel chose that moment to burst into the room with a small butler hanging from his arm. Both men looked most aggrieved.

'He wouldn't let me back in,' Adriel said, just as the man barked to Josie, presumably mistaking her for someone of higher social standing: 'I found this miscreant attempting to enter the property!'

'It would appear he already has, Jacob,' a new voice boomed. The voice of an upper-class ostrich, with undertones of furious peacock. 'And I would say he has more business being in this room than you do.'

A strange atmosphere entered the room with Countess May Damsell-Brownfield, one that had an equally strange effect on her unfortunate staff. Making no attempt to stand, the maid instead shuffled backwards out of the room, head bowed low, dragging the tea tray with one quivering foot like some prostrate serf fearing the landowner's cosh. The little butler not only ceased dangling from Adriel's elbow, but instead became consumed with the desire to smooth every crease out of the photography apprentice's jacket, even though this was an impossible task when it came to fabric gathered round a flexed joint.

'Thank you, Jacob. THANK YOU. JACOB.'

He gave Adriel's sleeve one final desperate smooth and then backed out of the doorway bowing and babbling his apologies until the door slammed, leaving them with only the countess's icy silence. She stood in front of Josie's carefully arranged scene, taking it in, emitting coldness and magnificence like a frozen star. Josie and Adriel exchanged a worried glance. Josie took a breath, preparing to explain that it was generally better to wait until the final panorama was arranged and photographed before making any judgements, and that while being in a room with the corpses of one's recently expired loved ones may be distressing, the ensuing image could be a source of comfort and delight for many years to—

'Very good. Continue.'

The countess turned and swept out of the room, leaving Josie and Adriel to their macabre but necessary work.

*

Josie eyed the cake stand's prettily decorated sweet treats, trying to work out whether the hazelnut meringue Genoese offered a better cream-to-sugar ratio than the cherry-topped sponge fancy. Probably either would be too unbecoming to eat in the countess's presence. She wished Adriel had taken cream tea with them rather than being forced into lemonade and cigars in the orangery with the butler, who was still keen to repent for last week's impropriety. It was difficult to be anything other than becoming with Adriel around, large and unruly as he was.

Speaking of unruly, the Damsell-Brownfield children burst into the room, each riding an expensively carved hobby horse with a long mane which Josie suspected was human hair. The countess followed just behind, cheeks pink, a few wisps of hair escaping the tight fretwork of pins Josie knew lurked beneath the pile of curls.

'I'm the winner of the National!' the young boy announced on completing his circuit of the table. Tripping over his hobby horse's trailing stick, he tumbled face first onto Josie's skirts, burying a mouth moist with milk and a nose dripping with far worse in the folds of crinoline. Josie froze, unable to help the child up, unable to do anything but suppress the urge to gag.

Apparently unaware of Josie's discomfort, the countess took the chair opposite, lifting the prone child into her lap in one fluid movement. The little girl, who had paused in mute horror at her brother's stumble, now resumed her own trotting circuit, tunelessly singing 'Ride a cock horse' as she went. Josie was for once glad of the restrictive nature of her corsets as they went some way towards steadying her roiling stomach.

'Will you not take some repast, Ms Loddington?' asked the countess, smiling indulgently as her little boy grabbed a coconut tartlet in each fist and crammed both into his mouth at once. Josie looked from his disgusting crumb-covered face to the obscene Turin Shroud snot-print on her skirt and selected the largest chocolate Bismarck on the plate, heedless of the dusting of cocoa powder it shed the moment she picked it up.

'I will confess,' the countess continued once Josie was engaged in devouring the chocolate treat, 'I have an ulterior motive for calling you back here.' A clot of cream coated Josie's mouth and she could do no more than gulp and nod. 'We were of course delighted with how the photographs came out. Some of the copies have been sent to the count's family in Dorset – his aunt commented that you made him look more dashing than he ever did in life.' The countess pinched a crumb from the tablecloth and dropped it back onto the cake stand. 'But then, she always was a sour old bitch.'

Josie smiled around her Bismarck. Perhaps she had misjudged the countess.

'Bitch,' echoed the little boy brightly. He'd somehow finished his double tartlet mouthful already.

'Now shush,' the countess said. 'The thing is, I did a little research into *your* research.'

Josie's jaw stopped working. She swallowed the last of the Bismarck and wiped the cream from her mouth with the back of her hand without thinking.

'So I know about your little pet, and I was wondering if you might be able to do the same for the children.' The countess covered the boy's ears for a moment. 'Losing their father *and* the dogs on the same day has been very hard for them to bear.'

'Daddy!' wailed the little girl from under the table where she had crawled, forgotten and with no one to cover her ears. 'Dumpling! Sausages!' She burst into tears.

'The dogs,' the countess explained softly.

'Your Honour, I absolutely cannot,' Josie began. 'Prince Soggy Bottom was a frog and therefore his physiognomy was far simpler than—'

'Prince…?'

'The pet. And that was many years ago and he did not survive the process for long and…'

The countess looked very sad, and a little of her coldness returned, but it was different this time, like an emptying winter bathtub.

'I understand,' she said. 'Of course. Jacob will see you out.'

She left the room with a rustle of skirts. Feeling guilty, Josie sucked the last of the cocoa dust from her fingers, wiped them off on her dress and stood.

'Please, Mrs Lady.' A small hand appeared from beneath the tablecloth and grasped the hem of Josie's dress. 'Please bring me my Dumpling back. I loved him like you loved your Prince Ploppy Pants.'

'Soggy Bottom,' Josie corrected automatically.

*

Josie carefully ran a scalpel down the length of the small, furry body. She could give them a taxidermied gift if nothing else – that was what she kept telling herself. But her gaze kept returning to the box of Prince's replacement parts, some rejected as too large for a frog, but perfectly acceptable for a dog...

She dropped the organs into the metallic dish at her side, marvelling over their colours and textures as she always did. As beautiful and varied as the countess's cakes. She hesitated over the heart and brain, wondering whether they would be better served remaining— no, no! They had to come out; it all had to come out. She should just strip the skin and have done with it. She had already built the skeleton. Most taxidermists twisted crude frames from wire, but Josie preferred something more robust, carefully assembling old mechanical odds and ends into a skeletal likeness of the original animal. The handle of a cane became a femur curving gently towards the hip joint, which was fashioned from an inkwell. The spokes of a bicycle Adriel had written off riding vigorously down a cobbled hill formed the ribcage, while the pedal of the same bike formed the basis of the skull.

'I have your earthworms.' Adriel burst in unannounced, causing her to drop the scalpel into the organ dish with a clang.

'Thank you, Adriel – just leave them there.'

Adriel hesitated in the doorway, holding the glass jar of wriggling worms as if it were a live grenade. He looked from the dish of offal to the metallic skeleton to Josie.

'Everything okay?' he asked, prompting Josie to wrinkle her nose at the Americanism. She didn't know where he got these things.

'It's fine, Adriel, really. I shall be up for tea shortly—'

'Is that my bike?'

'It was. Now it's a dachshund's skeleton. Now go, go!' She bustled him bodily out of the room, taking the jar of worms from his hand as she did so. Once she was certain his heavy footsteps had receded, she pulled back the curtain beneath her workbench and crouched in front of the vivarium. An excited *ribbit* issued from within the den of leaves and mosses as she dangled an earthworm inside. There was a whir of clockwork motors, a rustle of undergrowth, and the earthworm disappeared from her fingertips.

*

Dumpling's bark was made from the bicycle horn, which he could compress with the motors in his throat when he wanted to make a sound, which was apparently all the time.

'I can take that out for you—' Josie began as Dumpling chased the children round the hearth rug, honking away.

'Not at all,' the countess said loudly over the cacophony of honking, squealing and laughter. 'It's so wonderful to hear them laugh again.'

The little dog skidded to a stop and looked up at Josie, tongue lolling. He really was an excellent piece of work. She just hoped that her preservative techniques were sufficient for his eyes and tongue not to rot out over the coming months and years. Any internal bits were much easier to keep running, as they could have a constant supply of fluids and kinetic currents, but it was difficult to get the same effect in external components.

She held out the box of assorted tools and tinctures.

'The spray is for his eyes and tongue. It's just a mild saline mixture – Jacob should be able to procure more for you at the chemist with ease. That really is the most important thing to remember – spray twice a day, or if ever his eyes look dull. And if he' – she lowered her voice, mindful of the children – 'rips or tears anywhere, send for me immediately.'

The countess took the box, her gaze still firmly fixed on Dumpling.

'Actually, Ms Loddington, there is one more thing...'

Josie stiffened. She had been prepared for this. That was the problem with people. They always wanted more.

'As Adriel explained to you on my behalf,' said Josie, 'Sausages had undergone too much... trauma to be... useable.' It was difficult not to go into detail, but she'd rather the countess didn't put too much thought into which bits of her pet were mechanised and which were reanimated flesh. Josie knelt and stroked the soft ginger head, feeling the ridges of the pedal's edge beneath the fur.

'Yes, I know. It's not Sausages I'd like you to work on.'

Even though Josie knew the realities of Prince Soggy Bottom's workings, she often told herself it was all magical clockwork, a clever trick like the movements for the photos. She'd hoped the countess would do the same. It seemed she had, since she still harboured this foolish idea that Sausages could also be—

'Not Sausages?' Josie straightened, spinning towards the countess with such alacrity it set Dumpling to honking all over again. 'Your Honour, if you are suggesting what I believe you to be suggesting, then I really must advise you to desist with such thoughts! Put such notions aside for good and be satisfied that your children's grief has been lessened a modicum.'

The countess turned the full force of her stare on Josie.

'The Registrar of the General Medical Council is a personal friend.'

'Is that a threat?'

'Consider it an opportunity.'

'I am not a doctor,' said Josie, her voice slipping to a tone she usually only used when Adriel had done something really stupid like cleaning the camera lens with a scratchy cloth rather than the soft downy one specifically intended for the job. 'Nor do I ever intend to be, so anything the Registrar may have to say to me is by the by.'

The countess's expression was as stiff as her dead husband's had been all those weeks ago.

'Very well. Then you may consider our business concluded. You will receive the remainder of your payment in due course.'

Josie nodded, too furious and horrified to say anything further.

'He smells like mothballs!' the little girl giggled as the door slammed shut.

*

The countess was true to her word. The money was wired direct to Josie's account within a couple of weeks. It was a lot. Far more than she had been expecting. She almost contacted the countess to check if there had been some kind of mistake, but then she remembered that cold, stiff glare and it made her shudder. Instead, she bought a new carriage, a larger one with more space for all her photographic equipment, and a second horse to pull it. And a new, bigger vivarium, because she might get a new frog, she'd told Adriel, and he'd raised his eyebrows and asked why he was still procuring earthworms if there was no frog in the current vivarium. She told him he'd misunderstood and she'd meant in addition to that existing and perfectly normal frog, but immediately went out and bought him a new bicycle too, just in case.

For many months their business prospered and Josie focused purely on her photography, putting the taxidermy aside, because truth be told, the business with Sausages and Dumpling had put her quite out of sorts. She even photographed the occasional living animal to help recalibrate her mental well-being, but no living people, because they made such disagreeable models.

She was returning from one such job, having spent many hours trying to get a particularly languid Persian cat to open its eyes for more than a millisecond. Tired and cat-scratched, she was more than a little put out when the carriage lurched to a halt with such force that her newspaper was tossed from her hand and out the open window, and she came very close to banging her head on the opposite wall.

'ADRIEL!' she shouted, propriety flying out the window after her newspaper. 'HAVE YOU TAKEN LEAVE OF YOUR—' And then she saw it. A large stately coach blocked the road ahead, the coachman engaged in some kind of altercation with the proprietor of a street wagon, the kind with large wheels and a flat base, usually purveying foodstuffs of some kind. This one smelled of hot toffee and caramel, so Josie supposed it sold sweet apples or confectionery.

Adriel appeared at the window. 'They're holding up the traffic.'

'I can see that, Adriel. Pick up my paper while you're there.' She took it and hopped neatly out of the carriage. The horses waited quietly, far more patient than Josie herself.

'What seems to be the trouble?' she asked the coachman. It appeared he'd been waiting for this opportunity and was eager for the chance to recount his tale at length, with much gesticulation. Within seconds, Josie had the gist of it – the coach had bumped the confectionery wagon and the proprietor expected recompense, even though there was no physical damage to man, wagon or goods. Josie waited for him to reach the end of his monologue and as she did so, her eye roved across to the coach. It was large and grand with an extravagant coat of arms – a dormant ostrich between two rampant peacocks. Josie felt oddly cold and uneasy, though she couldn't be sure why. Then, as the coach's occupants leaned over to the window to see the reason for the hold-up, she knew. It was the countess, and a male companion. His skin was waxy and his mouth open in a terrible fixed grin, his eyes glassy and wrong. They moved, but without seeing. When Adriel touched her elbow, Josie gasped, startling the coachman into silence with the sharpness of it.

'We'll wait here until you're ready,' she told him breathlessly, allowing Adriel to lead her back to the carriage, half lifting her into the seat.

'Did you see him?' she whispered. He only nodded briefly and returned to the driving seat.

*

For a long time, she watched the cobbled streets slide past the window and listened to the comforting sound of the horses' hooves, only occasionally monitoring the spread of the dark patch on her skirt as her tears continued to drip into it.

'That work's not like yours, ma'am,' said Adriel. Josie jerked upright, wiping her eyes. She'd been so absorbed in her own pitiful horror and self-loathing that she hadn't noticed the carriage come to a standstill. They were home.

'It's not,' Adriel persisted. 'That was a monster. You make miracles.'

Josie sighed. She wasn't sure she agreed, but she appreciated the sentiment. It wasn't the first time she'd considered getting rid of Prince Soggy Bottom. It unnerved her, how well he was doing, how he showed no sign of rusting, or slowing down, or stopping, ever. She wondered what would happen to him when she wasn't there to feed him worms or clean out his vivarium. Would he become a terrible, waxen thing like the count? She couldn't imagine Prince ever being so unpleasant, or Dumpling either. And yet she couldn't be angry at the countess, not really. Wanting more time with a loved one was understandable, even if that time was a falsehood, a trick like her photography, like her taxidermy.

Adriel was still waiting, watching her, the concern on his large, broad face growing by the second. What could she do but keep on keeping on? More living, that was the answer, the only one available, to her and to Prince Soggy Bottom. More living with someone warm and alive to show you how.

'Tomorrow,' she said loudly, forcing brightness into her voice, 'you can coat the plates yourself AND put them in the... well, you can coat the plates. You'll like that, won't you, Adriel?'

'If you say so, ma'am.'

'I do, Adriel. And...'

'Yes, ma'am?'

'Perhaps we could go for a bike ride too?'

THE WHISKY SITUATION

There are worse things in the world than cloning whisky. Cloning people, I reckon, but in the eyes of the law, they're the same. Whisky, people, pedigree Shih Tzu puppies, so long as you're popping out copies using molecular cloning techniques, they'll all earn you the same stint. It's not that they actually think they're as bad as each other, I reckon. More about the fact both could send our economy, such as it is, into freefall. Copying grain for whisky, it's not like copying a baby, but imagine if you copied grain for food. Where would they be then, those rich bods who dole out food and work and housing?

We're sitting with one of them rich bods right now. Hair piled up all fancy, clothes with no visible seams. Makes me feel weird about my hair, my clothes. Lolly doesn't seem bothered. Got her pitch figured out.

'Before you taste it,' she's saying, holding up an index finger, keeping the whisky just out of reach, 'I want you to imagine the grain's journey. Ripened slowly in the sunshine, mixed with purest Highland spring water, in our antique copper stills.' The woman's closed her eyes now, like she's really seeing it, really experiencing the whisky's so-called life story. 'And then into the casks, beautiful age-old casks that travelled back from the Caribbean in the hold of a pirate galleon.' Pirates, is it? Last time it was a triumphant general returning from a naval battle. 'And then, after a long sleep, soaking in all that glorious swashbuckling flavour, we bottle that whisky in glass made by blowers from these very streets and deliver it to your door, so you might taste history.' Lolly whispers the last, and 'might' isn't a possibility but an absolute.

The woman opens her eyes. Looks at the whisky reverently, as if she believes all that is true. And it could be. The whisky's amber-gold and when you sniff, it smells of somewhere warm and distant, but the taste – not that I've ever tasted the genuine article, mind – is just a tiny bit off. Which is why you got to make them taste it with their imagination, Lolly says. Paint them a picture and they taste that instead of the inside of a laboratory pipette.

Good at painting pictures with words, our Lolly. Which is fortunate.

*

The factory was louder than you'd expect. How can a covert and illegal business carry on with so much clanking and whirring of machinery? How come everyone in the neighbourhood doesn't call the rozzers? Cos everyone's equally shady, I suppose, in an area like that. Bit different to our last suppliers, despite the virtually identical industrial estate. Clean and modern, this place, all the machinery built for purpose instead of tacked together from odds and ends dragged back from the tip. Going up in the world, Lolly reckoned. Loads more workers, and not the lecherous old lushes we were used to. Youngsters in lab coats, all with an unnerving sameness to them. I tried not to look at their faces too much, though – better not to be able to pick them out of a line-up, I always find.

Centrifuges spun and distillation units dripped and I wondered, not for the first time, how this could possibly be cheaper and less time-consuming than making the genuine thing. I guess it's to do with the batch sizes, and no government taxes like the legit distilleries have to pay. We used to be in the puppy trade, but it didn't sit well with me, people buying them by the crateload. Seemed people were finding their own way round the rationing, if you catch my meaning. No, whisky's definitely better.

Another lab coat, this one topped with glasses, approached us. He was holding a tablet, which immediately set alarm bells ringing in my head. Tapped in our order and got us to sign for it, which had me even more nervous, not that we'd used our real identities. When we're selling whisky we're always George Sisters' Distillery, even though we're not sisters and neither of us really knows the first thing about whisky. But we do know how to make a good impression.

*

When we're convincing new buyers, Lolly does the stories, and I do the presentation. You've got to spend money to make money, so each bottle is individually boxed in a genuine antique wooden case sourced from a legit local antique dealer.

Well, mostly legit. Always has more stock in after a church has been fleeced, but I don't think too hard on that. He knows what we're looking for now, so he keeps them aside when he finds them, knows we'll give him a good price. They got to be wood, and they got to have a nice lining, silk or velvet, or something else soft and shiny, but the outside can be a bit beaten up. In fact, it's almost better if it is. Helps Lolly's stories along if the case gives her something to go on.

We got a couple of street kids who fetch our bottles for us. Root around in the rich bods' bins and if they get caught, they just say they're searching for food and look all pathetic. Not hard when you're five stone, wet through and live on stale bread toasted in a burning bin. Some of them get lashes for it, and I always pay them anyway when that happens, even though Lolly reckons that encourages them not to look too hard. Brave words from someone who's not so much as had her ears flicked.

I've got a proper artist who paints the labels, working girl from canal-side trying to earn her way off the street. Was a watercolourist before the government made it harder and harder to make that kind of work pay. Never understood why they hate paintings so much. Where's the harm in pictures of the way things were? Not as if pictures can change anything. Except minds, I reckon, which I suppose is where the harm is.

And the part of it that drives Lolly crazy, that makes her think I'm out of my mind, is we only sell to one buyer a month, and whatever quantity they ask for, we halve it. Lolly thinks we're doing ourselves out of cash, but we still make a tidy profit, and she can't seem to grasp that nothing costs so much as rarity. We couldn't charge the price per bottle that we do if just *anybody* could get their hands on our whisky. And if ever funds run low, we sell it by the cup down Flea Alley and pretend it's just regular moonshine. Worst we'd get for that is a few weeks' hard labour.

*

The lady's hands are so soft and clean – she's never done a day's labour in her life, hard or otherwise. Got all her nails and everything. She holds the glass up to the light and swirls it, watching the glow from the chandelier reflected in the golden eddies.

'We'll take eight casks,' she says, regarding me with cool eyes that aren't used to being told no. Maybe that's another reason I always halve it.

'Can do you four,' I say. 'Fifty per cent cash deposit secures.' Key similarity between the likes of us and the likes of her – we all prefer to deal in cash.

The lady's eyes flash.

'My husband is a cabinet minister,' she says, quietly, like she's proud and ashamed of it at the same time. 'He has some very influential friends who—'

'Done,' says Lolly, holding out her hand. The lady looks at it.

I look daggers at Lolly, but she's wearing her Kevlar vest of stupid and taking the lady's money.

When we get outside, it's not just the air that's cold and brittle.

'What the hell are you doing?' I hiss, pulling myself up into the front of the carriage. George is stock still in the traces, his steaming breath the only clue he's genuine rather than synthetic. 'We don't have eight casks! We got six at most, and Franklin only found us packaging for four!'

'So we buy more whisky at the factory and pick up some old barrels at the docks. Stop making something out of nothing.'

That's exactly what I'm going to have to do, thanks to her.

*

I'm pleading with Rondel, one of our bottle-hunters, when the pigeon arrives. It lands on George's harness and one of his ears twitches back towards it – about the biggest reaction you're likely to get out of our George.

'I can't go back to the bins so soon,' Rondel's protesting. 'With dogs and security bots and the like it's a risky business anyway, even more when I were only there last week and chances are they won't have drunk all their booze in that space of time.' He's right, of course. Even rich bods place limits on their excesses. Sometimes.

I reach for the pigeon, knowing it's from Lolly before I even press the button on its leg. Rondel rattles on about how the nano walls are getting harder to hack and some people have gone back to standard walls because not all de-atomisers are compatible with them anyway... I wave him to silence. The recording device buzzes and hisses, distorting Lolly's voice, but not so much that I don't want to kill her.

'Sooooo... don't freak out. Factory's been raided. But we may still be okay. Rozzers took all the techs, but none of the tech. You get yourself down here quick, we can probably cook up some whisky. How hard can it be, right?'

'HOW HARD CAN IT BE?!' The pigeon flutters to a higher perch, startled. Rondel's laughing, and I clip him round the ear. 'Just get the bottles,' I tell him, readying George to leave.

If we don't sort out the whisky situation, I'll need something to club Lolly to death with anyway.

*

The factory's not looking so swish without all the lab coats running things. I'm not sure how much damage was done by the rozzers and how much is thanks to Lolly's failed experiments. She looked pretty guilty when I asked if the centrifuge was already like that when she got there.

'I found some manuals,' she says, handing me a tablet. 'Maybe you can make sense of them.'

'Oh, I'll sit here and read, shall I? Just sit and have a nice read until the rozzers come back and arrest me for disturbing a crime scene?'

'I'll keep watch,' says Lolly cheerfully, pulling herself up onto a countertop so she can see out the window. She idly pulls a wall-mounted keyboard down towards her and accesses the security system so she can keep an eye on all the entrances. Amazing how she can manage that, yet reading a manual's too much like hard work.

I study the manual for some time, but it's not much use. There's plenty of information about how the machines work, but it assumes its users already have sound knowledge of how to DNA profile the original samples and extract the desired essence. I tell Lolly her plan's a bust.

'I thought it'd just be like on the shows,' she says. 'You press a button and it makes a copy.'

'It sort of is,' I say. 'But we don't have anything to copy.'

'We have our whisky.'

'A copy of a copy? Lolly, that's weak, even for you.'

'You'd rather we go back on our deal? Fail to deliver to Mrs Poshnobs and her parliamentary husband?'

That's the problem with rich people. They're always connected.

'I suppose it's got to be worth a try.'

Sighing, I head back out to the carriage to pick up a cask of our finest.

*

'DNA extraction failed,' says the posh-woman machine voice. Lolly presses the button again. 'DNA extraction failed.' Press. 'DNA extraction failed.' Press. 'DNA extra— DNA extract— DNA ex—'

'It doesn't matter how many times you press it, it'll fail! It failed the first time, it failed the thirtieth time, it's always going to fail!' This is always the way with Lolly, always. I can't bear it.

Lolly shrugs. 'So we go round and tell the lady we can't get as much as we thought. What's the worst that can happen? She badmouths us to her mates at cocktail parties? We sell in Flea Alley a few extra weeks? It'll be fine.'

My shoulders sag. I hate making the business look bad and I hate how Lolly messes up all the time and it's always fine. But I don't see many options right now, so I wipe my prints off the tablet and Lolly's off the wall-mounted keyboard and head out to the carriage once more.

'Lucky no rozzers came, at least,' Lolly says, pressing her thumb to the scanner on George's harness to unspool his reins.

I open the carriage door and a particularly fat pigeon swoops out, startling me. It's shat all over the interior, floor to ceiling. I'll be recording a message of complaint for when it gets back to its handlers, filthy little git. It lands on top of the open carriage door and bobs its head stupidly, waiting for someone to activate its message.

'Fine,' I snarl, pressing its leg button harder than necessary. It pecks me and glares with baleful red eyes the whole time the recording plays.

'This is a message for Mrs Serena Bernhardt from Detective Superintendent Wesley of the Stoneybridge Road Constabulary with regards to your associate Mr Rondel... Dick.' Lolly snorts with laughter. I elbow her into silence as the message continues. 'Mr... Dick... was caught trespassing in the grounds of Cardinal Fettiplace's mansion. Due to the recent attempt on the Cardinal's life, this is being treated as a potential assassination attempt. Bail is set at eight thousand pounds. Failure to produce bail will result in Mr Dick's deportation.'

'Ha, Rondel got them to officially call him Mr Dick!'

I stare at her, horrified that any associate of mine could be so grievously thick.

'Lolly, Rondel's going to get deported unless we can find eight grand!'

'But his surname's Cunningham...'

*

I watch George, solid as a rock, hooves rooted to the spot until I give the command. I wish Lolly could be more like him. She's perched on the carriage with her hands jammed between her knees, juddering against the cold. And maybe with nerves. I don't exactly love this idea, but what else can we do? The man's a whisky connoisseur and that means he'll have the good stuff. He's also super rich, which probably means he won't miss the odd litre. If we don't sell him the whisky, we don't get the money and if we don't get the money, we can't get Rondel out. And there's no way I'm letting that kid get deported on account of us. I know what he was running from and there's no way he's going back to that if I can help it.

'Shall we, then?' I ask, pulling down my balaclava.

'I guess.' She puts hers on. It's bright yellow.

'Leave it off.'

She doesn't need telling twice, throws it onto the seat beside her.

'C'mon, then,' I tell her, twisting my flashlight until the light is dim but useable.

The cellar is dark, but it's got none of the dampness of our usual underground haunts. It's lined with varnished wood, shiny under the torchlight and cool to the touch. There's a wall of bottles with foreign labels, glass glinting midnight red. I assume it's wine. Lol reaches for a bottle but I stamp on her foot and she withdraws her hand.

'Focus!' I hiss.

In the opposite corner, there's the special stuff, wooden boxes and gilt cylinders that I know will contain single bottles of spirits worth more than our entire haul. But that's not what we came for either. We came for the casks. There's so many, stacked in a corner; his wife wasn't lying. Makes me wonder at the kind of parties these posh nobs might have, getting maudlin on fancy liquor in their velvet drawing rooms as they light cigars with rolls of cash.

Our casks aren't so big, but they're deceptively heavy and an awkward shape, like a fat puppy that doesn't want to be picked up. Once we've decanted a bit of the fancy whisky into them, it takes two of us to carry them, heaving them back up and out through the hole we hacked in the nano wall, out to George, into the back of the carriage and repeat. On the third go, when we're puffing and sweating in our dark robber clothes and I'm thinking of saying to Lol that the next one will have to be the last, George snorts and pricks up his ears. I heft my latest cask into the back with a strength born of fear and climb up on the top of the carriage to peer out through the fog. It's a real pea-souper, but even I can make out the red and blue lanterns twinkling in the distance.

'Rozzers!' I say to Lol, sliding down into the driving seat. 'Get the nano-hacker.' For once she doesn't argue and disappears into the murk, returning with the little silver box a moment later. I stuff my robbing gear under the seat and try to look normal as I click my tongue to George. He clops off down the street, hoofbeats deadened by the fog.

*

'We can't do it.' Lol chews on the skin at the sides of her nails. Cautious, now it's too late. Typical.

'We're doing it,' I say. 'Rondel's not going down under on our account.'

'There's rozzers outside!'

She's right, and truth be told, I'm sick with fear. Their carriage is parked outside, and there's more of them milling round the driveway, ominous shadows in the morning mist.

'And we're making a delivery. A pre-agreed delivery. Can't arrest us for that.' And it's true. I've been through it in my head over and over. So long as the security system tripped out like it was supposed to, there's no way for them to know we stole the whisky. And who'd be brazen enough, idiotic enough to sell the whisky straight back to them? And even if they tested the whisky, what would they find? Not that it was cloned, because it came out of those expensive Scottish casks, still safely nestled in that fancy cellar.

I've purposefully layered up so the cops won't think it's too weird I'm sweating cobs. Weather's cold, but I'm in the sheltered driving seat in my scarf and wool coat and fur-lined cap with earflaps. I loosen the scarf a little as I rein George to a halt behind the police wagon. A young 'un's barring the gate, and I try my best to look the flustered delivery driver as I approach her.

'What's going off? Got a delivery for 'is Lordship and 'er Ladyship.'

She shakes her head. 'No deliveries.'

A local girl, I can tell. Eyes like that, I wouldn't be surprised to find she's a Miller, or a Munson. Two families so intermingled as makes no difference. But it's more than that, it's how at ease she is standing there, how unconcerned she is by me. Out of towners, they fill their pants as soon as a local approaches 'em. Get all twitchy and keep their hands in their pockets to be sure we're not rooting round in there. She's just keeping an eye on me, sensible. I can work with sensible, I reckon.

'Look,' I say, quietly so she has to lean in a little. 'We're both just doing our jobs here. And we know the lord likes his drink, we know that, right?' She smiles at that, so I press on. 'And my life won't be worth living if I don't get this latest batch to him for his parties or whatever he gets up to.'

She's laughing now, openly laughing. I take a step back, half expecting her to clap handcuffs on me without missing a beat, but she doesn't. Just grins and says: 'I'd hawk yer booze somewhere else, love. His Lordship's not going to be needing it.' She shakes her head. '"Whatever he gets up to"!'

'What's going off?' asks Lolly, as I climb back into the driving seat. Police officers file out, carrying boxes filled with papers. Who has papers these days? Posh nobs, apparently. Guess you can't hack paper, at least.

'Dunno,' I say, fiddling with George's reins for as long as I can as I peer across at the house, trying to fathom what's going on in there and if it's anything to do with us. 'But we need to find another buyer.'

*

It's not so hard when you've got a quality product, and this time we had for real. Turned out the Cardinal was a mite jumpy what with all the attempts on his life, and some more whisky was just what he needed to calm his nerves. By mid-afternoon we'd made enough for Rondel's bail plus a few weeks' board and food for ourselves and George. Can't say fairer than that. We figured we'd pop over and pick Rondel up on foot, give ol' George a break and buy some of that street food Rondel loves so much.

We arrive at the police station with paper bags dripping grease and wafting the smells of warm onions and battered turkey legs with each step. There's an old boy on the reception desk, reading a newspaper and sucking one side of his luxuriant grey moustache. He hastily removes it from his mouth as we approach.

'I'm here to pay bail,' I say. 'For Rondel... Dick.'

Lolly tries to hide her snigger in a mouthful of fried onion, but I catch it and elbow her sharply. The copper doesn't notice, though, and goes off to find the relevant datacard in the storage cabinets behind him. I concentrate on my turkey leg, thinking if moustache-sucker don't hurry up, there's going to be nothing left for Rondel by the time he gets out. Hope he had a good lunch of prison gruel.

A commotion in the doorway makes me turn, chin greasy with turkey juices. Several burly constables are manhandling a dishevelled fella between them. Very well-to-do, nice grey pinstripe suit, shoes I could see my face in if I was so inclined, not the sort you usually see cuffed and stumbling through the station. He seems as surprised as I do, bellowing to anyone who'll listen in a cut-glass accent: 'This will not do! Unhand me! The House of Lords shall hear about this!' Behind him, there's the woman, still in seamless clothes, hair still piled up but some spilling out now. She's not handcuffed, just walking meekly between two more officers, her eyes downcast so she don't see me, too caught up in the shame of the moment. And that's when the farthing drops.

'They will 'ear about it, mate,' says the nearest constable, amusement brightening his rough, ruddy face. ''Ouse o' Commons, too. They'll all be talking about you and your cloning. Booze AND people? Press'll 'ave a field day!'

Lolly's gorming open-mouthed, treating everyone to a look at her mushed-up onion.

'Fill in this form and scan your card at the bottom.'

'The factory—' Lolly starts, but I elbow her extra hard as I take the tablet from him and she coughs and splutters, fighting to swallow her snack.

By the time Rondel's alongside us, crouching to rethread his bootlaces, they're taking his Lordship's prints and he's lost some of his bluster. Maybe some laws are the same for all of us. I hope that's true, at least. Rondel don't notice any of that, straightening his back and saying bold as brass: 'Met some right thirsty coves in here, and with money to burn. What's the whisky situation?'

TOTAL TRANSPARENCY

The first inkling we had that something was wrong was when her belly turned transparent. I drew back the covers and rolled over to kiss her tummy as I often did in the mornings, but this time recoiled in horror. Her soft pink guts were on show, glistening wetly like coral. Once the panic subsided and my breathing eased, I realised it must simply be a dream, and sat watching her sleep, waiting for us both to wake up. But the waking never came and eventually she mumbled: 'What are you doing? I'm cold,' and tried to pull the duvet back across her exposed midriff.

She reacted calmly to the revelation when I pointed it out to her. Her face was impassive as she looked down at her lower intestine, visibly squeezing in peristalsis. 'I suppose we should see a doctor,' she said eventually, and began putting on clothes. I was relieved when her T-shirt covered this new window on to her insides, but tried not to let it show on my face.

'Doesn't it hurt?' I asked. And: 'Shouldn't we call an ambulance?'

She shook her head. 'Don't make a fuss,' she said. 'I'm sure it's nothing.'

*

The doctor didn't know what to make of it. 'Asymptomatic, you say?' he said, scratching his head. He took down a fat medical textbook from his shelf and leafed through it. Called in the nurse from the next room, the phlebotomist from upstairs, the student doctor from across the hall. None of them yielded any answers, only further questions. My wife's skin was still there, and perfectly fine – smooth to the touch, unblemished. Just not visible. Each of the medical professionals wanted to touch it and they palpated her abdomen while staring directly at the insides squishing around beneath their fingertips. When they looked at each other, their eyes shone. There were some serious publications in this, and they all knew it.

I hated to see her poked and prodded so, but it didn't seem to bother her, so I kept quiet, just gave her hand a squeeze every now and then, regular as peristalsis.

'We'll do some blood tests,' said the doctor with a quick nod to the phlebotomist. 'Rule a few things out.'

*

Two weeks later, her condition had worsened. The transparency had spread. Her intestines, stomach, liver, spleen and kidneys were all invisible too now, along with all the musculature and bone of her abdominal and lower-back muscles, meaning that when she stood before our front window, if I angled my head right, I could see directly through her to Mrs Parker's curtains twitching across the street. I drew our own curtains in response. Our dog, a black and white spaniel with a constantly wagging tail, barked at the sudden movement.

My wife shushed him and looked at me sadly. 'Don't want the neighbours looking at the circus freak?' she asked.

I kissed her forehead. 'Don't be ridiculous,' I said. But it wasn't so ridiculous. She looked like an unfortunate magician's assistant, cut in two but miraculously walking about.

Word got out. When I drove her to the shop to pick up toiletries and sugary biscuits to help replenish her after the constant blood tests, or when we took the dog out for a walk, people stopped in the street trying to get a glimpse of the vanishing flesh. Even when she wasn't with me, I was the partner of the vanishing lady, so I warranted a good gawk too.

The tests had ruled lots out: necrobiosis lipoidica, argyria, macular amyloidosis, any condition that might make the skin thinner or the tissue abnormal. But they had ruled nothing in. 'As long as it doesn't hurt, I'm sure it's fine,' my wife kept on saying whenever I cried.

I still kissed her belly. It was hard, being unable to see it, but easier than when I had been able to see her slowly digesting last night's fish and chips.

*

Within a month, the condition had spread to her chest. Seeing her beating heart and flexing lungs was unsettling, but it was what was no longer there that was truly upsetting. The little mole on her ribcage that I loved to tickle, the rise-fall of her breasts when she was sleeping. Now just an empty space. The doctor wanted to take her on a medical tour. I tried to dissuade her, thought it sounded like the kind of freak show no longer indulged in modern times, but she said it was only for medical professionals, and if someone could learn something it would be worth it.

I tried to get the time off work to go with her, but I found it difficult to explain the nature of the event, and why I needed to be there.

'So, your wife, she's sick?' my line manager asked, concern in her voice.

'Yes… no… not really. That is, she's okay within herself.'

My line manager had only ever seen my wife meet me in the car park, wrapped in her long coat, her disappearing parts covered with thick black wool.

'Well, yes, she did look fine when I saw her last,' my line manager said thoughtfully. She would probably have signed the paperwork if I'd pushed it, but to be honest, it seemed like my wife didn't want me to go with her, and I'm not sure what use I would have been. And anyway, the only thing that ever made the dog's tail droop was when we left him in kennels. I couldn't do that to him, not now when his daily routine was already in such turmoil. He wanted her walking him, not me, and he whined and pulled for home as soon as we left the house. But he had to be walked, and she couldn't do it, not in her condition. So I stayed, for him.

How I wish now that I had gone, if only to see a little more of her.

*

When my wife returned from the tour, I could tell she was in high spirits. I was in the middle of trying to poach eggs, her favourite, and was at the tricky point where I couldn't take my eye off them for even one second, so I let the dog rush to greet her and listened appreciatively as she shouted through while she hung up her coat and put away her boots. She alternated between making a fuss of the dog and telling me about her trip. 'Oh, such a good baby, how I've missed you! I met so many specialists you would not believe! Yes, you are a good boy, and so shiny! But all of them said they'd never seen anything quite like whatever I have! Don't jump up now, there's a lad. I met a boy from Botswana with translucent hands and feet, but that was as close as we came to finding anything similar.'

The 'we' stung a little – a word that usually included me, and this time didn't. But all of that was forgotten the instant she joined me in the kitchen.

The entire top of her head was missing and I could see the kitchen cabinets behind her, starting to yellow with age. Her eyes, her wonderful eyes, always so warm and full of love – I could never look in them again, and never again know that she was looking at me. I could see in the deep V of her turquoise shirt that her collarbones had gone too.

'Oh, sweetheart,' she said, folding me into a hug as I wept. 'Focus on what's here, not what's gone.' She took my hand in hers. They were still there, nails bitten down and dirty like always. You'd think she was a farmhand, not living a life of leisure as a medical marvel. She kicked me lightly in the shin, and there was her foot, her toenails painted, which wasn't like her at all, but when she saw me staring quizzically at them, she shrugged the shoulders of her shirt and said: 'I got bored on the road.'

She kissed me on the lips, with her lips which were still there, and I closed my eyes and held her and imagined the rest of her.

The dog whined at our ankles and the eggs hardened on the stove.

*

'You may have to face the reality,' the doctor told me solemnly later that week, 'that your wife may eventually disappear completely.' I suspected my wife had already been told this news, and had accepted it, because she'd slipped out a moment before to take a birthday card upstairs to the phlebotomist. She was good at that now, slipping away unnoticed; her clothes were taking on her invisibility too.

'I can't,' I said, not recognising this defiant voice coming out of my mouth. 'I won't. There must be a cure.'

The doctor sighed heavily. 'There's make-up we could use,' he said. 'Total cover-up. She'd never look like she did, but you'd be able to see most of her extremities. But,' he held up a finger to keep me from rushing off, as he could see I was desperate to go and get some for her right there and then, 'it has already been offered to your wife, and she has already refused.'

I sat back down heavily. 'Refused?' No, there must have been some mistake. Perhaps she was worried about the cost? She hadn't worked for some time now, and my wages weren't the highest. But whatever it was, we'd find a way to get her that make-up. We'd crowdfund it if we had to.

'I'll talk to her,' I said. 'I'm sure she'll want it.'

*

'No.'

'No?'

I could tell she was ruffling the dog's ears by the way they were moving around, but her hands were all but gone now. Occasional glimpses of the blue-green veins of her wrists were the best I could hope for. Her lower legs fared a little better, the ankle bone still prominent, and the arch of her foot. The big toe on her left foot, and the pinkie and its neighbour on the right. There had been no real rhyme or reason to her disappearance, except that it had spread outwards from those early beginnings in her belly.

'Why not?'

'I tried it during the tour. It made me look frightening, like a waxwork come to life. This is better, really.'

It's not better for me, I wanted to scream, but I knew it wasn't about me. That's the worst thing about your loved ones having a condition like this. Nothing can ever be about you. Well, not the worst thing. But the worst thing you can bear to think about.

*

Once my wife had gone completely invisible, it was beyond awful at first. I'd pace from room to room, calling her name, terrified that she had left me. She seemed to have more fun with the phlebotomist than me these days. They'd drink cocktails together and whisper. The phlebotomist was better at behaving as if the invisibility were normal, but that's easier to do when you don't have a history to compare things to.

And so I'd fantasise that she had slipped away, and they were somewhere without me, sharing secret, invisible moments.

The dog could always sniff her out, though. He'd charge around with me, nose to the floor, and bark when he found her.

'Why didn't you answer?' I'd ask her. 'I was calling you – why didn't you answer?'

'I'm just always so tired now,' she'd say. 'And I don't hear so well anymore. I'm sorry, my love.'

'You must never apologise,' I'd tell her, and with the dog's help I'd find her hand and hold it, and he would lie with his front paws propped up on her, looking like he was levitating his own head.

The doctors couldn't do any further tests, because they couldn't find her veins, or her ears, or her open mouth when she said 'AH', so there was no way of telling whether this new lethargy was caused by the invisibility, or just another disease.

But we got by, and when she was feeling up to it, we'd chat. Sometimes I'd try to keep her talking as long as I could so I could enjoy her voice, but then I'd feel guilty for being so selfish and wearing her out. Often I'd show her photos of our wedding, or holidays, or nights out with old friends. She didn't always comment on them, so I couldn't tell if she was looking at them or not, but I enjoyed seeing her in them if nothing else.

*

It was as winter rolled round again that the dog began disappearing too, even quicker than my wife had. His tail was the first thing to go. I could still hear that he was wagging it furiously, because it would thwack against the rug in the front room, or the tiles of the kitchen floor, but I could no longer see it. His ears went next, which caused lots of concern at the park. But once they realised whose dog it was, the other dog walkers seemed unsurprised, as if it was obvious whatever my wife had was contagious.

I didn't think for one second that it was, as the vet had said it was highly unlikely that my wife's invisibility was communicable to dogs. It was just an unfortunate coincidence. But a tiny bit of me hoped it *was* contagious, because then we could all be invisible together. I would hear the other dog walkers muttering: 'First the wife, and now the dog, poor thing.' I'm not sure whether the 'poor thing' was me or the dog, but neither of us appreciated the pity.

I thought my wife might be upset that the dog was going invisible too, but she was delighted. 'Oh, look!' she said. 'His ears are just like mine!' And of course, I couldn't look at either his ears or hers. Ever again. Who would have imagined missing someone's ears? It just isn't something you think about. I must have looked sad, because she touched my hand and said: 'It's not so bad, you know. I was never one for mirrors anyway, and not being able to see my own legs? It's like I can fly now!' I quickly put my hand over hers to make sure it was really there. It was – I know it was.

*

Of course, I don't see either of them at all now. They have both disappeared completely. The phlebotomist doesn't come round for cocktails anymore. I still roam from room to room now and again, calling her name and the dog's as well, and worrying that they've both left me. They had lots of TV offers before their respective conditions got too bad – maybe they belatedly accepted one of those and are now living invisibly in a big new house without me. If I happen to see the dog walkers, they tell me I should get out there again, meet new people, buy a new dog. But they don't understand.

Some mornings, I will see the muddy pawprints across the kitchen tiles, or hear a distant bark right at the bottom of the garden where he's found a squirrel. Or some evenings I'll come home and find she's left my favourite book on the table for me to reread, or put my slippers by the radiator so they're warm for my feet.

I still have a dog. I still have a wife. They're just invisible now, that's all.

THIS TIME, FOREVER

1966

She had a flower in her hair the first time he saw her. Everyone had a flower in their hair, but she was different somehow. The other girls were all blondes and redheads and brunettes, skin sun-darkened from running around nude all the time. She was pale, the flower a bright orange gerbera, like a ball of flame against her glossy black hair. Her dress had billowing sleeves and a cinched-in waist, orange and blue. She ran with the others, danced with them, but she wasn't like them; he could see that even from a distance. He wanted her, but not in the usual way.

He wanted her forever.

He watched her for a long time. She twirled and twisted gracefully to the music and when a shirtless boy offered her a pipe, a phial of powder, a handful of pills, she shook her head each time and carried on dancing. He liked that. Usually they were so weak, such followers, such sheep.

As the sun dipped lower behind the stage and people lit torches and bonfires all across the campsite, he moved closer, edging out from beneath the spread of the oak tree. He mingled with the crowd, fitting in easily, matching their movements. After studying them so long, it wasn't difficult.

He managed to be alongside her as the song ended. Watched as she whooped and applauded, jumped up and down and whistled at the man on stage. She blazed with happiness. He wanted a share.

For something to do he took a roll-up out of his pocket and put it in his mouth, fumbled in his pockets for a match. Then he remembered she hadn't accepted anything, not even the pipe, and took the roll-up back out of his mouth again, threw it on the grass. He heard laughter, a gorgeous, weightless sound, and realised she was watching him.

'Just remembered I quit,' he told her shyly, eyes on the ground. What was wrong with him? He was never shy.

'That's refreshing,' she said, smiling and coming closer. 'No one seems to deny themselves anything these days.'

He locked eyes with her and felt a rush of cold blood down his spine. It was like she was challenging him, like she knew who he was and what he was about, and was daring him to try something else instead. He wished he could, but it wasn't that simple.

The music started up again and her eyes darted away from his, back to the stage, then found his face again.

'Come on,' she said suddenly. 'Let's try and get to the front.' Grabbing his hand, she led him through the crowd and he followed meekly, like a sheep. Or perhaps more like a lemming.

1967

There was a full moon the night they did it. There didn't have to be; he just thought it made the occasion more romantic.

Returning to the place where they met wasn't essential either – it just seemed right.

There was no festival at this time of year. The field was silent, stretching for miles, the grass made grey by the twilight. Grey for her at least. For him it was as green as on that day. Everything was the same, all the colours singing, vibrant. He even asked her to wear the same dress. She did. She wrinkled her nose at him and rolled her eyes, but she still put it on.

They walked hand in hand to the oak tree, the place they'd shared their first kiss. They kissed again and the intensity was still there, her eyes, her touch, her scent commanding all his senses. He lowered her gently to the grass, and she let him lie on top of her, willingly.

He'd told her it could wait, that they didn't have to do it now, that she would be beautiful to him no matter what. But she turned eighteen next week and she was terrified of getting left behind, so it had to be now, she said, it had to be before she was officially an adult.

He nuzzled her neck, smelled her hair, intoxicated. At the last moment, he pulled back, stared into her eyes, asked for the millionth time that spring: 'Are you sure? Are you sure you want to do this?'

And she gazed up at him, the moonlight turning her skin porcelain, and she sighed and said, 'Yes, I'm sure. I love you.' After a pause, after he hesitated, she added, 'Do it already!' and they both laughed.

So he lowered himself down into her, gently pinning her down, trying to keep her still and quiet as he did it, because they had to be quiet, couldn't get caught by some farmer checking his fences or someone walking their dog.

They did it, knowing that everything would be different, but hoping it would all stay the same.

1974

That was when the cracks first started to show, she always thought. It had seemed so exciting when she was a kid, running away with him. Seeing the sights, seeing the world. London, Milan, Paris, Tokyo. There was nowhere they couldn't go, no one they couldn't be. Leaving her family had seemed a small price to pay for all those opportunities. Back then.

Now she didn't have any family. Just him, and whoever they were tagging along with at the time. He'd said they were a community of sorts, these others, these hangers-on, but most of the time they didn't feel like it. They weren't like him. They were selfish and cruel, only out for themselves, only hanging out because they could get something out of the arrangement for the moment. Then they were gone again, often for years at a time.

He'd explained to her that she only felt the way she did because she didn't go way back with any of them like he did. That once she'd got used to things, she'd establish the same kind of rapport. So far, that hadn't happened.

And now here they were, back in England again, in a poky café in Camden, again. Everyone was talking and smoking and she hated it. He was lounging by the wall, talking to two girls. Both had long white-blonde hair and brightly coloured head-bands. Twins or something.

Lazily she made a fist and imagined pounding their pretty little faces to mush. See how he liked that. A public scene. Oh, how he hated public scenes.

When he came back over she pretended to be reading the menu. He smirked.

'Thinking of ordering something?'

She narrowed her eyes. Even if she could, she wouldn't eat the shit they served in here. 'No.'

His smile faded.

'What's wrong?'

'Why do you always make a beeline for their kind?'

'What do you mean, "their kind"?' He pulled up a chair, tried to take her hand, but she snatched it away.

'You know what I mean.'

He did know what she meant. She could tell by the way he looked away before exhaling. Exhaling! Even that was fraudulent. After a while, he shrugged.

'I just like talking to them is all.'

'You used to like talking to me.'

He opened his mouth, then shut it again. She waited, but he didn't say anything else.

1985

She checked her hair in the mirror, chewing gum. She'd found that gum could stave off the hunger. Gave her fringe another quick comb. She'd always known the mirror thing had to be a fallacy. How else did they always look so good? Now the proof was right in front of her. She slicked on another layer of lip gloss, smirking at the colour's name. *Artery*. One last look at her flawless skin. Strange how she almost craved a wrinkle.

She strode onto the dance floor, glancing around for a likely lad. Or lass. It didn't really matter. A bloke with a slicked-back quiff and braces was trying desperately to catch her eye. She relented and went over.

'Evening,' she said, trying to keep the boredom out of her voice. Not that enthusiasm was important. He'd come with her anyway – they always did. She barely bothered with the preamble these days.

'You're gorgeous,' he told her, voice thick with alcohol.

Oh, God. The desperation came off him in waves – would have made her nauseous if her stomach hadn't been empty and growling.

'Um, yeah,' she replied, forcing herself to lie, 'you're pretty cute too.' *Pretty ugly. What you mean is pretty ugly.* 'Why don't we go somewhere more private?'

He looked like he might wet himself in his excitement. She hoped he wasn't drunk enough to actually do that. That would be embarrassing. Steeling herself, she took his hand and led him back towards the toilets.

As she was about to push the door open, she took a final look around, just in case there were any bouncers watching. Bouncers could be a real pain in the arse. But she didn't see any. What she saw was... him... standing by the bar, arms folded, looking straight at her. She dropped the drunk's arm like it was a crucifix. Drunky looked puzzled, pawed at her with his big sweaty mitts, but she easily shrugged him away and started towards the bar.

She almost stopped herself when she saw the girl by his side, a big-eyed, big-titted redhead, drinking a cocktail through a curly straw and looking at him like he was her god. Then the anger and the hurt rose up in her and she propelled herself forward with sheer will alone.

He didn't look surprised, or happy, or angry. He didn't look anything – he just looked. Now she was in front of him, she didn't know what to say. She wanted to take him in her arms and cry into his chest, but she wasn't about to do that. She wanted to scream at him and throw his girl's drink in his face, but she couldn't bring herself to do that either. So instead she just indicated the girl with a cock of her head and said, 'So this is your idea of a break, is it?'

'What about your guy?' he countered. She looked back over her shoulder. The drunk had followed her partway and was standing on the steps up to the bar, frowning, torn between her and dancing to Morrissey.

'What do you think?'

'How do you know I'm not in the same boat?'

'You're supposed to be on the wagon.'

'Because you said you admired self-denial.'

Her heart swelled until it hurt. Why did he have to remember everything? He always remembered every little detail and used it against her. Unless... she breathed in unwillingly – such a silly throwback to her old life – unless he remembered because it mattered to him. Could it? Did it? Did she still matter?

'I— I just don't understand why you always need to be near them,' she stammered quietly. 'None of the Community do.'

'And we both know how much you love the Community.' He stepped closer and took one of her hands in both of his. Leaned close to her ear, so that all the hairs prickled on the back of her neck. 'It's because they're happy with what they are. Like you used to be.'

She drew back, gasping, outraged. Her mouth formed words that wouldn't come until she managed to splutter: 'But I did this for you!'

'Well, maybe you should have done it for you,' he told her sadly.

1998

He drummed his fingers on the table and checked his watch again. Looked out through the dusty window and wondered why he'd picked this place, this bijou Camden café. She'd never liked it here; she probably wouldn't even show up.

He sipped at the coffee he'd had to buy. It wasn't like it used to be in here. You couldn't come in just to smoke and hang out with musicians. You had to actually buy drinks or food, or the staff got all antsy.

He thought he maybe should have met her in a pub instead. True, most of the ones in London had at least a couple of Community members in them, but there were few places in the capital they didn't frequent. That was the problem with all the major cities. Why hadn't she just let him take her out to the country like he wanted? He'd picked her because she seemed like that kind of girl.

The bell over the door rang as someone came in. He looked up, excited, but it wasn't her. Just some old lady with a fur coat and a sour face. He lowered his eyes back to his coffee cup.

Yes, they should have met up in the Speckled Hen. She might have liked all the corny horse brasses over the bar and the dusty Victorian bed-warmers in the windowsills. Last time he'd been in there was to talk about her, so it would have been fitting. He'd met up with a leading Community member, one of the real old-timers, nearly a thousand years old, or so everyone said. He appeared in his early forties, silver-haired and striking in a classic-movie-star kind of way.

The old-timer had sat and listened to him speak and then looked at him with a mixture of pity and admiration and said, 'Eternal love's a nice idea, but it doesn't work, son. Ask anyone in the Community. They've all tried it. Friends with no ties works best for us. It's the only way for folks with our longevity.'

And he'd nodded and pretended to concede to the wisdom of all those centuries, while thinking: *You're wrong. It will work for us. It will.*

The bell clanged again, but he was lost in his coffee cup, right until the chair by his side scraped back and she sat down.

He felt his face split into the broadest grin, couldn't stop himself blurting joyfully: 'You came!'

She waved him to silence.

'We need to talk.'

2003

He felt like a stalker, and it wasn't a nice feeling. He'd never felt like that watching her before she knew him. He'd felt romantic and desperate and secret. Now he just felt seedy. But she hadn't called. She'd said she would call when she was ready for them to make a real go of things, and she hadn't called and he'd waited years. Literal years.

He watched her cross the road. She wore a long grey wool coat and high-heeled boots. Her hair was long and wavy now and she wore oversized sunglasses to fend off the bright autumn sunlight, but otherwise she was the same. Exactly the same – perfect in every way. He hid behind a parked car when she glanced over her shoulder, fully aware that he was acting like a lunatic.

He just wanted her to understand. She'd never understood. She thought he'd picked up a human toy and dropped it when it became something else. He hated that she thought he was as faddy and fickle as the others, moving on from one plaything to another.

He wasn't, he wasn't. It took him a moment to realise where the wetness on his face was coming from. He even looked up at the sky to see if it was raining before he realised he was crying.

He laughed bitterly. Look what she'd done to him. He wiped his eyes on his sleeve. No. That wasn't it. She was right – he never wanted to take responsibility for anything, always living in a dream world.

Look what he'd done to *himself.*

2066

She stroked the racer suit thoughtfully, smoothing it against the muscled contours of her stomach before swinging a leg over her bike and flicking it to drive. They didn't make loose-fitting day clothes anymore; it wasn't the fashion for people her apparent age. Still, she'd shopped around until she found a racer suit in blue and orange.

She rounded a corner, leaning with the bike as it thrummed along, engine purring, water vapour rushing out the exhaust. She checked the time and distance again on her watch. Plenty of time.

Plenty of time! The concept made her laugh. She'd made him wait decades. What if her time had run out? What if the final vestiges of his love and humanity had turned to dust and she was on her way to meet some savage-eyed creature? She couldn't really blame him if that were the case. It shouldn't have taken her so long to sort everything out in her head. She had always felt the same; it should have been simple.

She indicated to overtake a transport convoy, swinging past the long trail of armoured vehicles and taking the next exit.

On the other hand, how could it ever have been simple? How could a seventeen-year-old be expected to plot their whole future after one whirlwind year? They'd both been ridiculous idealists, but he seemed different now. More grounded. Patient. Perhaps…

She reached her destination, turned off the navigation system and stayed sitting on the bike for a moment, thinking. Mind made up, she sighed, got off, reached for the container on the back of the bike. She pressed the buttons and it hissed open. Feeling slightly stupid, she removed the orange gerbera. It had cost a fortune and would be dead by the end of the day – beautiful, fleeting, silly thing that it was.

She twined its thick, furry stalk into her hair regardless.

Straightened her back.

This time, she told herself, when she saw him approaching on the horizon, raised her hand, mirroring his wave, his smile. *This time, forever.*

PHOENIX

Sym stared into the open pit of the hearth. Nothing but ash and dust; a few lumps of kindling turned to carbon. And yet he couldn't stop staring. A vortex seeking to suck him in.

Four days now he'd sat in that armchair. He'd moved a couple of times, of course. Sipped a few mouthfuls of water from the rain butt outside, retrieved the last hard crust of bread from the cupboard and returned to his seat to gnaw at it like a rat. For the first couple of days he'd stooped over the rain butt to wash and afterwards had run a comb through his hair. A pointless ritual.

His eyes flicked to the mantelpiece, as they were wont to do. He couldn't look at the urn, wouldn't. He refused. But his sadist eyes determinedly steered his attention back to the burnished brass handles – representations of long, curled feathers – and the lid, an ornate dome engraved with a flaming heart.

Typical of her to choose something so quaint and ostentatious. Typical of her to choose the thing at all. He'd told her it was morbid, strange, upsetting to him for her to do so. But she had just tilted her chin downwards in that way of hers, like she was trying to hide her amusement. Her eyes were dark and bright, like a deer's but without a trace of fear.

'Don't be silly!' she'd scolded him. 'Nothing morbid about it! It's wonderful.'

Wonderful.

Even in his thoughts he spat the word.

His friends had warned him against her. They had been right, he supposed – just not in the way they thought. They'd assumed her fey ways and childlike obsessions wouldn't mesh with his determined restraint and desire for order. But she had opened him up to a world he could scarcely have imagined. With her, he could hear the hollow voices of the trees, see the sentient movement of a sunbeam when it thought you weren't looking, taste an approaching storm on the wind. And now she was gone, and it was like his senses were dulled. Aged before his time, hearing failing, eyes dimmed, taste diminished. He clenched his fists against the musty arms of the chair, releasing dust into the stale air, trying to get back to the present, but his sadist eyes were matched with a traitor brain, forever returning to the least-wanted memories.

They'd only been together two months when she first got ill; he realised that now. He should have seen the signs. A once-voracious eater reduced to pecking at crumbs. A lively, eloquent talker suddenly quiet and reflective. But he'd been so wrapped up in adoring her, those changes didn't occur to him until she collapsed.

As she hit the floor of his mind's eye, he jolted to his feet. He was breathing heavily, hot knives of pain stabbing up and down his spine. No doubt from the shock of the sudden movement after so many hours inert.

The urn was in his hands, though he couldn't remember picking it up. He toyed with the lid, running his fingertips round the outline of the heart.

No.

Better get a fire going.

He was surprised to find it was dark outside. Approaching the fifth day then. Only two days left to decide. If what she'd told him was true.

How could it be true? It was crazy. She was a hedge witch, he knew that, but this was something else. Far beyond coaxing a bird into telling you where the sweetest blackberries grew, or catching starlight in a pebble to make a lantern. This was old and dark and frightening.

If it was true.

Outside again, staring at his reflection in the rippling surface of the rain butt. He looked old and worried. Leaning over, he splashed a little water into his face. The woodpile was low. He should chop more. But that meant going into the woods, leaving the armchair, and the fireplace, and the urn.

Leaving Phoebe.

There, he'd said it. Thought it, at least. He couldn't leave the cottage as long as Phoebe was there, even if she was just a memory in an urn.

He picked up an armful of logs.

When he returned to the cottage, it seemed darker and colder than before. Throwing the logs down, he brushed the bark dust and twigs from his sleeves. Patted his pockets. Where was that damned lighter? He could really use one of Phoebe's sparks right now.

He was suddenly hit by an image of her, crouched before an

unlit campfire, radiant in the twilight. She pressed the sticks together and they flared to life. She smiled at him knowingly and he loved her so much it hurt. The memory struck like a fist, pummelling him in the stomach, in the heart. He fell back into the armchair, overwhelmed with grief.

The urn was in his hands again. He twisted the lid off. There she was.

It didn't look how he'd expected. Bright turquoise, mottled with navy-blue flecks. It almost glowed, nestled in the darkness of her ashes.

He knelt at the hearth, instinctively shaping the logs and twigs into a rudimentary nest. He tipped the egg out carefully. It filled his palm and was hot to the touch. He brushed the ashes from it and tipped them back into the urn.

He looked from egg to nest and back again. Should he start the fire first, or would the egg do that itself? Should he do this at all? It was the stuff of nightmares. People didn't come back, and if they did, they were changed. Soulless wraiths. Ghouls. Monsters.

He stroked the egg, imagined smashing it on the stones of the hearth. The thought made him sick.

He was bombarded with a sudden flurry of images. Phoebe dancing, skirt twirling and snagging on briars; Phoebe falling back into the soft autumn leaves laughing, flailing her arms and legs against the leaf litter to make a 'leaf angel'; Phoebe rubbing a frozen chick between the palms of her hands, breathing into its tiny beak until it squeaked and scurried back to the coop. He realised he'd been gently massaging the egg like that chick and smiling. He'd thought he'd forgotten how to smile.

Very gently, he placed the egg in the centre of the kindling nest and returned to his armchair to watch.

ACKNOWLEDGEMENTS

My heartfelt thanks to all those who have published and championed my writing over the years: Writing East Midlands, particularly competition judge Jacob Ross, who said *Sidhe Wood* was 'weird', but to 'just keep going' anyway. So many people have been kind about *Ghillie's Mum* I'm sure to forget someone, but Will, Janet and Emma of Commonwealth Writers in particular, Luke and the rest of the team at *Granta*, all of those involved in the BBC Short Story Award and the ALCS Tom-Gallon Trust Award (particularly my fellow shortlistees), and those at Galley Beggar Press who gave helpful feedback on the ending when it received a special mention in their competition. Several stories (*Dead Men Don't Count*, *A Winter Crossing* and *Frozen*) were given their first chance in the world by Murder of Storytellers and I'm very grateful to all the amazing editors there, particularly Jack, Shannon and Adrean for their insightful advice. Rupert and Miles of TSS Publishing for including *Grandma's Feast Day* in their beautiful volume of Cambridge Prize shortlistees. David and Andy at the New Accelerator for taking *Blanks* despite its strange length and POV. Jason at PunksWritePoemsPress, which, though sadly no longer active, produced some wonderful titles, including a collection containing *Mrs Sutherland's Arms*. David and Rory for publishing *Something or Nothing* in the NTU commemorative anthology, but also all those others who said kind and encouraging things about my writing during my time on my MA and PhD – Sarah, Phil, Georgina, Anne, Jo, Becky, Richard and of course the incomparable Graham Joyce and his equally marvellous wife Sue.

All at Fairlight naturally have my undying gratitude for publishing both *Dreaming in Quantum* and *Beyond Kidding*: Louise, Urška, Lindsey, Bradley, Laura, Joanne and Mo in particular plus those adjacent to Fairlight such as Mark for his artwork. Thank you so much for all your hard work, and for never recoiling in horror at the earlier versions my fevered brain put in front of you.

I suppose I can't really have an acknowledgements section without also thanking my family – hopefully there aren't any moments you'll have to warn your friends about in this one. And Ant, without whom none of this would be possible.

Previous Publications: *Sídhe Wood* – published in the 2017 East Midlands Aurora competition's (digital-only) collection, *Cut the Clouds*; *Ghillie's Mum* – published in *Granta* July 2018; Adda Stories September 2018; Comma Press September 2019; broadcast on BBC October 2019; *Frozen* – published in *Faed*, Murder of Storytellers; *Dead Men Don't Count* – published in *The Misbehaving Dead* by Murder of Storytellers; *Grandma's Feast Day* – published by TSS Publishing January 2020; *Blanks* – published in The New Accelerator; *Mrs Sutherland's Arms* – published in 2016 in *Don't Open Till Doomsday* by PunksWritePoemsPress, now OP; *A Winter Crossing* – published by Murder of Storytellers; *Something or Nothing* – published in *25* by Shoestring Press.

ABOUT THE AUTHOR

An award-winning short fiction writer, Lynda Clark has been widely published in anthologies. Her debut novel *Beyond Kidding* was published by Fairlight Books in 2019 and is in development for a feature with Film4. She has completed a PhD in Creative and Critical Writing and is currently a Research Fellow in Narrative and Play at the University of Dundee. *Dreaming in Quantum and Other Stories* is her first collection of short stories.

FAIRLIGHT BOOKS

LYNDA CLARK

Beyond Kidding

A darkly humorous, genre-bending work of literary sci-fi. Lynda Clark is a new talent to discover for lovers of Kurt Vonnegut and Douglas Coupland.

When Robert (or Kidder, as his best friend calls him) decides to impress at a job interview by making up a son, he discovers that maintaining the lie is far harder than he thought – so he invents a story that 'Brodie' has been kidnapped. After all, it's not like they're going to find the fake boy.

But a few weeks later, Kidder receives a call to collect his non-existent son from the police station – a boy who looks exactly like the picture he photoshopped...

'A dark and quirky debut – funny, sad, thought-provoking and unexpected.'
—Emma D'Costa, Commonwealth Writers

'I loved absolutely every moment of this book.'
—Liz, Bookseller at Indigo – Prospero Books

The Fairlight Book of Short Stories (Volume 1)

The Best of Modern-Day Short Story Writing

From flash fiction to mini-novelette, Fairlight presents twenty-four of its best short stories from some of the world's most talented new and emerging English language writers. Chosen from work sent to Fairlight over several years by writers around the globe, this anthology celebrates the art of the short story form: a vehicle with the power to delight, entertain or instantly transport the reader to another state, another world, another emotion.

Twenty-four stories by twenty-four writers, including various award-winning short story authors, and Women's Prize-longlisted author Sophie van Llewyn.

> 'Vivid and diverse, this is an admirable and highly enjoyable collection of new voices.'
> —J.S. Barnes, author of *Dracula's Child*